the next step. If not, you will have to listen to the whispers of the skeleton.

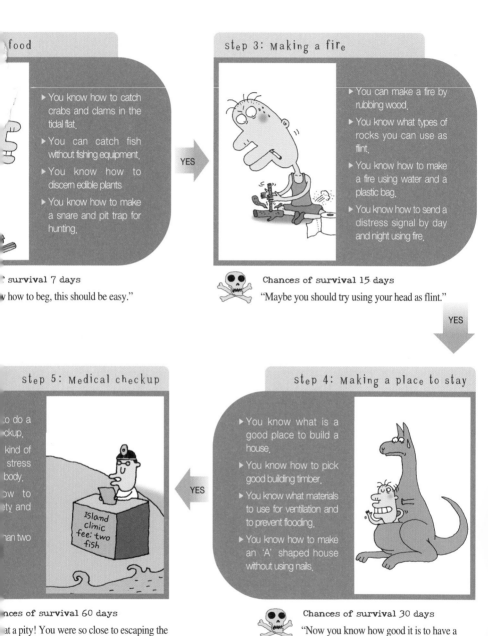

food

- You know how to catch crabs and clams in the tidal flat.
- You can catch fish without fishing equipment.
- You know how to discern edible plants
- You know how to make a snare and pit trap for hunting.

survival 7 days

how to beg, this should be easy."

step 3: Making a fire

- You can make a fire by rubbing wood.
- You know what types of rocks you can use as flint.
- You know how to make a fire using water and a plastic bag.
- You know how to send a distress signal by day and night using fire.

YES

Chances of survival 15 days

"Maybe you should try using your head as flint."

YES

step 5: Medical checkup

to do a ckup.

kind of stress body.

w to ty and

an two

Island clinic fee: two fish

nces of survival 60 days

at a pity! You were so close to escaping the d."

step 4: Making a place to stay

- You know what is a good place to build a house.
- You know how to pick good building timber.
- You know what materials to use for ventilation and to prevent flooding.
- You know how to make an 'A' shaped house without using nails.

YES

Chances of survival 30 days

"Now you know how good it is to have a place to stay."

* If you know how to do more than two things in each st[...]

step 1: Making drinking water

► You know the plants and animals that live near water.
► You know how to purify water using pebbles or sand.
► You can make drinking water from sea water.
► You know what to do when you lack drinking water.

stagger~

YES

Chances of survival 3 days
"Hurry, come lie down, the grass will be your blanket."

step 2:

Chances o[...]
"If you kno[...]

step 6: Making a raft

► You know how to transport wood to make a raft.
► You know how to tie the raft firmly.
► You know what shape the raft should be to minimize the resistance of water.
► You know what is good weather to set sail on the raft.

YES

Escape will succeed
"Bye. Visit again some time."

► You know how [...] basic medical ch[...]
► You know what [...] adverse effects [...] can have on your [...]
► You know h[...] overcome anxi[...] fear.
► You know more [...] medicinal herbs.

Cha[...]
"Wh[...] islar[...]

Test Your Survival Chances

You get on the plane looking forward to
your trip overseas.
How long has it been?
The plane begins shaking wildly
with a thunderous noise, as if doing an 'air stunt'
you tremble in fear until you finally faint.
You open your eyes and find you are
on an uninhabited island.
You have unwillingly fallen into an
unknown world.
Could you survive here?
Test your chances of survival.

If you can do two or more things in
each stage you can move on to
the next stage and your chances of
surviving until you are rescued will go up.
But if not?
Unfortunately you will have to
give up and listen to whispers of ghosts
who have gone before you.
Your game for survival begins on an island
where there's no 911 rescue team, no guardian
spirit and no passersby.
We sincerely hope you will pass the test
and become the indomitable island person⋯⋯.

Following Robinson Crusoe

Following Robinson Crusoe

Copyright ⓒ 2002 by Daniel's Stone Publishing Co.
All rights reserved.

Written by Sangjoon Park, Kyungsoo Park
Illustrated by Wooil Lee
Editorial supervision by Editorial Department of 〈Donga Science〉 magazine

Translation by Mikyung Shin
Translation supervision by Dr. Michael Holstein, Dr. Sandra J. Holstein

Daniel's Stone Publishing Co.
#396-22, Seokyo-dong, Mapo-gu, Seoul, Korea

ISBN 978-89-5807-214-0

로빈슨 크루소 따라잡기

지은이 박상준 · 박경수 일러스트 이우일 감수 과학동아 편집부

초판 1쇄 발행 2002년 12월 1일 초판 7쇄 발행 2008년 12월 30일

펴낸곳 뜨인돌출판사 펴낸이 고영은
마케팅책임 김완중 제작책임 정광진
편집장 인영아 기획편집팀 이경화 장은선 디자인팀 김세라 오경화
마케팅팀 이학수 오상욱 엄경자 최인수 총무팀 김용만 고은정

북디자인 하늘소 필름출력 다산기획 인쇄 예림 제책 바다

신고번호 제 1-2155호 신고년월일 1994년 10월 11일
주소 121-840 서울시 마포구 서교동 396-22(솔내 1길 16) 2층
대표전화 (02)337-0212 팩스 (02)337-0232
뜨인돌 홈페이지 www.ddstone.com 노빈손 홈페이지 www.nobinson.com

ⓒ 2002, 뜨인돌출판사
'노빈손'은 뜨인돌출판사의 등록상표입니다.
책값은 뒤표지에 있습니다. ISBN 978-89-5807-214-0

Following Robinson Crusoe

뜨인돌

People like uninhabited islands. They have a longing for it, even if they've never been there. It has a mysterious charm that tugs at the heart. Things such as the blazing sun, vast sea, thick virgin forest and wild animals come to mind. It seems like the place of thrill, romance and loneliness.

But what if you really ended up on an uninhabited island? There's no tap water or gas stove. Your cell phone won't work and you can't order food. Except for the soil, sea, plants and animals, there's nothing on an uninhabited island that you can use. You have to search for water and make a fire yourself. Would it still be so romantic then?

You have to be strong to face nature by yourself. It is the strength to make things using objects around you. The strength to get water from earth and fire from light. It is the strength to transform nature to meet human's needs. Science is the great wheel that led humanity to modern civilization.

Our hero is not a genius. Others know what he knows and he doesn't know what others don't. But he is very curious. He continually asks 'why?' to all natural phenomena. The moment common knowledge meets extraordinary curiosity, the uninhabited island becomes a big laboratory. All his actions become an experiment and science.

We have to learn. We have to learn from his curiosity that turns ordinary knowledge into a totally different result. Look around you. The sun that rises and sets everyday, the water you drink and fire you use everyday teach us so many things. Look how we have changed nature and nature has changed us. The path our hero took is the path humanity took during thousands of years. This is the reason our story takes place on an uninhabited island.

At a glance, science and an uninhabited island don't seem to go well together. But if you look a little closer you will see that the island will bring us endless joy and learning. On an island there is nothing finished for humans but there are so many things ready for use. Now let's start out. Let's start out in our venture to learn from the godfather of island life, Robinson Crusoe.

Summer of 1999
Jongro, Seoul

Contents

North Star! This is the northern hemisphere

Sending an S.O.S.

Let's go! Exploring the island

In search of a new home

Binson gets lost

Telling the direction with a stick

If only I had a magnet

Building a house

Island villa on the hill

Binson the Hercules

Fish lost in the maze

Binson goes gathering herbs

Toadstool or not, that is the question

Setting a trap

Binson's treasure chest, the tidal flat

Equipment for a cultured life

Binson gets meat and pelt

Making smoked meat

Blue days

Despair comes with fear

The fire dies

Sleepless on the island

Ahh! I can't see

Wake up, Binson

Binson gets back to his feet

Balance sheet of hope and despair

Aloe, the mysterious medicinal herb

Urine, a marvelous medicine

Three months have passed

Mirage on the sea

There is something beyond the horizon

Making a raft

Learning to forecast weather

Setting sail in search of hope

1

Morning on the strange island

Nobinson woke to cold sea water touching his face. He could not lift a finger, his body feeling limp like salted cabbage. "Naturally", "he thought to himself." "Sea water is salty." The pitch-black night, the frightening roar, the crash, the screams······ those horrifying moments began to drift back through his cloudy head.

---

limp (형) 축 늘어진
pitch-black (형) 칠흙처럼 어두운
crash (명) 부딪치거나 깨지면서 나는 요란한 소리
touching his face 분사절의 형용사적 용법으로 the cold
    sea water를 수식한다. 분사절은 touching이란 동사로만

이루어지지 않고 touching his face 전체가 분사절인 것에
    유의할 것
think to oneself 혼자(남몰래) 생각하다
frightening roar 무시무시한 굉음
drift back 뒤로 돌아오다(back은 부사)

He felt thirsty. The sides of his throat were stuck together, like a pair of inseparable love birds.

His mouth felt arid, as if it was full of sand. It was a terrible thirst, as if the last drop of moisture had dried out from his body. The blazing sun was stinging his skin like needles. Only then did he realize he had been swept by the waves to the beach of this strange island.

"I can't be the only survivor among those passengers?"

Still lying on the sand, Nobinson looked around him. All he could see on the wide beach were the waves coming and going, and absolutely no sign of another human being. A short distance away, a square tin swept onto the beach was glittering in the sun. Whatever was in that tin, it was now gone. It was also the only trace of the airplane.

"Water⋯⋯ I have to find water."

He staggered as he tried to raise himself. He clenched his teeth and stood up on the beach. It didn't matter where he was or how he was going to escape. What he needed most right now was water. He had already swallowed so much seawater and sweated so much that he could barely keep his eyes focused. He had to find water, somehow, before dehydration got any worse.

He opened the sack he was wearing on his waist and checked his belongings. Camera, pocketknife, lighter, a cheap raincoat, and a few plastic bags his mother had forced him to pack.

He also found his glasses with strings attached, a watch, some clothes, underwear, belt, shoes, and a wallet with some money inside. His knapsack would have come in handy, but he was lucky to have what he had now.

Something warm flowed down his face. He staggered away from the beach licking the salty liquid, not knowing or even caring whether it was sweat or tears. He started out in search of a drop of water to quench the deathly thirst.

sting (동) 찌르다
tin (명) 주석→깡통, 통조림
stagger (동) 비틀거리다, 흔들리다
clench (동) (주먹, 손 등을) 꽉 쥐다, (입을) 악물다
dehydration (명) 탈수
belonging (명) 복수로 쓰일 때는 소지품
glasses (명) 복수로 쓰여서 '안경' 이란 뜻이다
knapsack (명) 배낭
quench (동) 가라앉히다, 억누르다
stick together 서로 들러붙다
as if it was full of sand it = his mouth/ as if는 가정법을
    이끈다. as if the last drop of moisture had dried out
    from his body에서 보듯이 후자가 문법적으로 원칙이나

요즘에는 이런 원칙에서 벗어나는 경우가 많다.
Still lying on the sand 양태를 나타내는 분사절
It didnt matter it는 가주어, 진주어는 where ... 이하/ ...은
    중요하지 않았다
What he needed most right now는 관계대명사 what
    이 쓰인 경우이다. 주어로 쓰이기 때문에 물론 명사절이지
    만 관계대명사 what이 쓰인 관계절은 언제나 명사절이다
get + 비교급 : 더 ~하다 여기에서 any는 부사로 비교급
    앞에서 '조금이라도' 라는 뜻이다
get any worse 조금이라도 더 악화되다
His knapsack would have come in handy 가정법으
    로 아쉬움을 나타낸다

The Search for water

Binson mustered all his common sense to find water; Water always flows downward and gathers where the bottom is hard, and to find water in a mountain, you have to go to the valley; etc. But the valley he found was dry and all he could see were sand and gravel. He must have taken the wrong way. He muttered even in his blurry state of mind.

"If this were a video game, I would reload without saving."

He saw ants crawling up a tree. Startled birds scattered above the woods. Flies and mayflies swarmed around his face. His thirst was worse due to heavy perspiration, and dehydration was getting to his head now.

At last Binson gave up on finding water and collapsed on the ground. His eyelids were getting heavy.

Who could that be, that man wearing animal skin on his back like a

---

muster (동) 소집하다, 집합시키다.
mutter (동) 중얼거리다
blurry (형) 희미한, 더러워진
mayfly (명) 하루살이
swarm (동) 떼지어 날다
perspiration (명) 땀
urine (명) 소변, 오줌
muttered even in his blurry state of mind/ even은 전치사구를 강조해 주는 부사 / 몽롱한 상태에서도 중얼거리다

due to ~때문에. due to는 구어적 표현이므로 owing to, because of를 쓰는 편이 좋다
was getting to his head 머리까지 이르다 → 정신이 흐릿해지다
is comprised of ~로 구성되다 cf) be comprised in 에 포함되다
aqueous solution 물의 성질을 띤 액체 → 수용액
salivary glands activity 침샘 활동
resulting in ~결과를 나타내는 표현으로 (~으로) 끝나다, 귀착하다

Water, together with air, is most vital to any living organism. Seventy to eighty percent of the human body is comprised of water, and all metabolisms that sustain life take place through chemical reaction where various materials are dissolved into an aqueous solution.

The human body has about 45 l of water. About 2.75 l of that water is replaced everyday. Out of the total 1.5 l is from drinking, 1 l is from eating, and about 0.25 l is obtained through metabolism of dry food. About 1-2 l is discharged through urine.

If no food or water is supplied, the body breaks down fat to make about 0.25 l of water. But more is lost to respiration and perspiration. At least 0.4 l is lost just by lying down and doing nothing. In short, you always have a water deficit problem.

The least amount of water necessary to sustain physical functions is 1 l a day. At 86°F(30℃) it becomes 2.5 l, and at 95°F(35℃) 5 l. If there is a shortage of water, the hormones decrease the salivary glands' activity, resulting in a dry mouth and thirst.

The conclusion is simple. Humans cannot live only on bread; they need water too.

primitive person? Hey, he's also carrying a spear. I thought I was alone on this island. Is this a dream or what?

"You really don't know? Of course it's a dream."

"Who are you?"

"Me? I'm the original stranded island man."

"What? You mean Robinson Crusoe?"

"Binson, you really are mentally challenged."

"Why?"

"What do you mean why? If you dig down into the dry valley, there is water. Sand and gravel absorb water well, and you can easily find water below that. Also, if you dig where grass is growing, you will find water

spear (명) 창
strand (동) 좌초시키다 / the stranded = 좌초된 사람 → 무인도에 떨어진 사람
that be, that man wearing animal skin on his back

like a primitive에서 앞의 that은 대명사, 뒤의 rhat은 접속사이다. 따라서 앞의 that = that man wearing animal skin on his back like a primitive too. Not only that. When ants are climbing up a tree, they are most probably heading towards water.

If you see insects and birds, it means water is somewhere nearby. We humans are not the only ones that need water, you know."

"……"

"Now you see? You fail at being a crash survivor."

"Who is good at being a crash survivor from the start?"

"I was. I was good from the start."

"……"

"Well, I'll be going now. Look again Binson. Good luck."

"Wait! Wait a second. Please."

He flailed his arms, shouting as he woke up. He wished he could have gotten more information, but at least now he had a clue how to find water.

An hour later. Binson was deeply troubled. He had found water, thanks to Robinson's advice, but it was filthy. The puddle of water he had found between the rocks was filled with small worms, and the water under the sand without any bugs looked even more suspicious. The puddle he had found in the woods was crawling with snails.

It is natural that small bugs live in water that runs through forests or valleys. It is also natural that different kinds of organisms live in the water depending on the grade of the water. Binson had liked reading comics better than anything else since he was young. He remembered almost exactly what he had read from "Determining the quality of water by the creatures living in it."

First grade water : crawfish or shrimp. Potable without further processing.

Second grade water : ephemera larva. Requires deposition or filtration.

Third grade water : marsh snail, leech, water snail. Third grade water or below requires chemical treatment.

Fourth grade water : damselfly, larva of moth or flies.

Fifth grade water: mosquito larva or tubificid.

---

flail (동) 도리깨질하다, 마구 흔들다
filthy (형) 더러운, 불결한
suspicious (형) 수상한, 미심쩍은
puddle (명) 물웅덩이, 보통 물이 고인 곳을 가리킨다
crawl (동) 기어다니다
crawfish (명) 가재
shrimp (명) 새우
Potable (형) 음료로 적합한. 마실 수 있는
ephemera larva 하루살이 유충
deposition (명) 침전
marsh snail 다슬기 = a horn shell.
leech (명) 거머리
damselfly (명) 실잠자리.

moth (명) 나방
tubificid (명) 실지렁이
being a crash survivor은 동명사절이며, a crash survivor은 충돌에서 살아남은 사람, 즉 조난자
He wished he could have gotten more information 은 가정법으로 '~을 바라다, ~했으면 좋았을 텐데' 라는 뜻이 된다
even more suspicious even은 비교급을 꾸밀 수 있는 부사
It is also natural that~ 에는 should가 쓰이는 것이 보통이다. = It is also natural for different kinds of organisms to live in the water~

What he had found was unclean water of below third grade. Binson thought long and hard. A while later he jumped to his feet, hitting his knee, as if he had realized something. He cried,

"Water purifier!"

Making a dependable water purifier

What Binson had thought of was filtering the water. Filtering is passing liquid containing impurities and particles through a filter with small holes, separating the particles from the liquid.

He dug out the inside of a stump with his pocketknife and made a water container. He decided to use small stones, sand, and pebbles as the filter. But they were not enough to filter all the impurities. The water contained small particles that could not be filtered with just sand and pebbles.

"It would be great if there was some charcoal."

The surface of charcoal is filled with small holes that are 1/1000mm in diameter. Porous matter such as charcoal is excellent in absorption and is perfect for filtering impurities from unclean water. He remembered reading a comic book about the Chosun Dynasty where people put charcoal in the well to purify the water.

water (before purification)

rocks

sand

charcoal

sand

pebbles

<How to purify water>

Hehe, tastes great!

---

dependable (형) 믿을 수 있는, 믿음직한
impurity (명) (주로 복수로 쓰여) 불순물, 이물질
stump (명) 그루터기
charcoal (명) 셀 수 없는 명사로 쓰여 '숯'

diameter (명) 직경
Porous matter 다공성 물질
such as = like, for example

But there is no charcoal on this uninhabited island. Neither did he have the means of building a fire to start making some. After some thought, he finally decided to use his undershirt instead of charcoal.

"This will filter most impurities."

Binson filled the plastic bag with the water containing snails inside and poured it over the water container.

Then he gulped the clean water flowing out of the small hole below. Now that his belly was full of water, his mind cleared and he could see properly.

"Whew, that's much better. I bet even Robinson didn't know this."

It was the first time after the crash that he felt a bit relaxed.

Longing for Prometheus

With dusk the temperature dropped like a rock. He wanted to make a fire, but he had nothing to make it with. His lighter was wet with sea water and useless.

"If there were fire, I could boil water and cook some clams. There must be some way to make a fire?"

The first thing that came to his mind was a flint. He first gathered some dry grass and twigs to use as firewood. Then he picked out some hard-looking stones.

"People used to light cigars this way. I can do this."

gulp (동) 벌컥벌컥 마시다
flint (명) 부싯돌
uninhabited island 사람이 살지 않는 섬 → 무인도
most impurities 대부분의 불순물. 따라서 most는 many 의 최상급이다. 한편 most는 보통 관사 없이 쓰여 '대부분 (대다수)'이란 뜻을 갖는다
I bet (that)~ 틀림없이 ~이다: 반어법으로 쓰여 '아마 틀림 없이 ~하겠지' 라는 뜻을 가지며, 이때 that은 보통 생략된

다
With dusk 땅거미가 지면서 = when dusk was deepening
came to his mind 생각이 머리에 떠오르다, 생각나다
used to (조) 옛날에는 ~하곤 했다. 현재와 대비된 과거의 습관이나 상태를 나타내는 조동사로 그 습관이나 상태가 지금은 존재하지 않음을 나타낼 때 쓰인다

But the fire didn't start. No matter how hard he hit the stone there was no spark, just crushed bits of rock flying in all directions. He tried dozens of times, changing stones, but finally had to give up and decided to look for another way.

The second method he tried was rubbing wood together. He had seen primitives start a fire by rubbing a stick against a piece of wood in comics and films.

'Just because the flint idea didn't work doesn't mean I will fail again.'

But unlike his expectations, he couldn't start up smoke, let alone a fire. His palms were about to catch fire before he could make a real one.

After a lot of sweat and time, all Binson got were blisters. He threw away the piece of wood. He lay on the grass with a sigh, covering himself with the raincoat. He thought of the great Prometheus, who had given fire to mankind.

Learning the principle of distillation through dew

Dawn. Binson woke up writhing in pain. His stomach was boiling as if a volcano had erupted inside.

'What could be causing this? I haven't eaten anything.'

As he grabbed his stomach, the plastic bag and water caught his attention.

'Of course! It's the water. Filtering was not enough; I should have boiled it before drinking.'

At that moment, Binson's eyes flew open. He had felt moisture on the raincoat.

'What's this? Water? There's no sign that it had rained last night. Then what?'

Binson bolted to his feet and shouted.

"Dew!"

Binson thought long and hard about how he could gather dew. Dew that forms in the early morning evaporates too quickly to gather enough of it. He couldn't roam around the woods before sunrise to gather dew

---

crush (동) 박살내다, 부수어 ~이 되게 하다
distillation (명) 증류
writhe (동) 몸부림치다, 괴로워하다
evaporate (동) 증발하다 → (명) evaporation
in all directions 사방으로 = in every direction

The second method = another way (that he decided to look for)
should have boiled should have + pp는 '실행하지 못한 일에 대한 아쉬움' 을 표현한다. '~했었어야 하는데' 라는 뜻

either because he would use more energy than he would get collecting water. It would be a losing bargain.

'There should be a more efficient way to collect dew without having to move.'

A while later, his eyes twinkled, like dew.

"Yes, the vinyl raincoat!"

Vinyl does not absorb water, so he could gather dew from the surface. He would spread it where the ground is sunk in the middle and put a stone on it. Water would collect in the middle and wouldn't evaporate as quickly as dew. Then he would be able to get at least a couple of cups of water every morning.

When his thoughts reached this point, he dug out some dirt to make a slant and spread out the raincoat above it.

Now I will drink pure morning dew every morning.'

Content with himself, he suddenly realized that his stomachache had gone.

Changing the sand field into an oasis

Morning. Binson sat in the tree shade, immersed in thought. He had moistened his throat with the dew that had gathered in the morning, but obviously he wasn't going to obtain enough drinking water that way. He had to get enough to at least supplement what he would lose through sweat, let alone get enough to take a shower.

The sun was hot despite the fact it was early morning. His glasses became misty because of his sweat. A sudden thought hit him as he took off his glasses, mumbling. He stared hard at the mist on his glasses to grasp the lightning inspiration that had flashed through his brain. A little while later, exclaimed

"Let's try it!"

What had flashed through his head was the word 'evaporation.'

---

slant (명) 경사
immerse (동) 파묻히다. 열중하다
supplement (동) 보충하다, 보완하다 = complement
despite (전) …임에도 불구하고 =in spite of
misty (형)흐릿한 ← 안개가 자욱한 ← mist(안개)
mumble (동) 중얼거리다
lightning (형) 번개 같은

inspiration (명) 영감 →lightning inspiration 순간적으로 떠오른 영감
immersed in thought 처럼 수동태로 쓰일 때는 '~에 몰두하다' 는 뜻 = immersing himself in thought
let alone 보통 부정의 문맥에 사용되어 '~은 말할 것도 없이, ~은 물론'

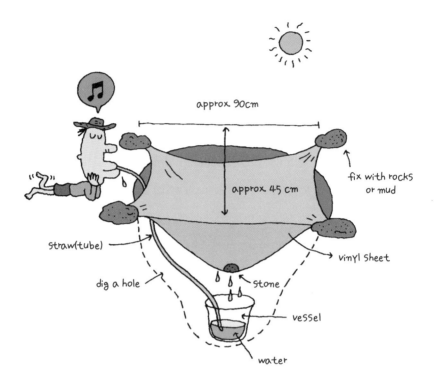

approx. 90cm

approx. 45 cm

fix with rocks or mud

straw(tube)

vinyl sheet

dig a hole

Stone

vessel

water

When the sun is hot, moisture evaporates. Then the air will be pregnant with vapor, and if he could find a way to collect that vapor, he would be able to get water.

But collecting vapor was the problem. He couldn't catch it with a net or grab it with his hands. Staring at his glasses, he finally came up with the idea of using a 'hole' in the ground.

"With the temperature so high, the water will evaporate from the sand. If I dig a hole and cover it with the vinyl raincoat, the hole will soon be saturated with vapor evaporating from the sand. And vapor can't pass through vinyl. The vapor will liquefy into water, and all I have to do then is drink it. I must be a genius!"

Binson started digging eagerly, not even caring how much he was sweating. Then he covered the hole with the raincoat and put a small stone in the middle. That way the water drops that collect on the surface would trickle to one spot. But then·······.

"You idiot! Are you that stupid?"

He started smacking his head with his fists. He had forgotten to place a container to hold the water inside the hole.

If he didn't have a vessel to hold the water, it would drip back into the sand. The survivor from a crash who was stuck alone on an island could not afford to let that happen.

He positioned the cup he had carved out of a piece of wood and put the raincoat in place again. He muttered as softly as possible, lest anyone

---

pregnant (형) 가득 찬(= filled), 임신한
saturate (동) ~에 충분히 배어들다(보통 수동태로 쓰인다)
liquefy (동) 물로 바뀌다. cf) LNG = liquefied natural gas 액화 천연 가스
trickle (동) 방울져 떨어지다,
smack (동) 때리다, 입맛을 다시다
drip (동) 떨어지다 → drip back into ~로 도로 떨어지다
Stare at ~을 응시하다(at 대신에 upon이 쓰일 수도 있다)

came up with ~생각해내다, 고안하다
the idea of using a hole in the ground 동격의 of가 사용되었다
could not afford to V ~할 여유가 없다
the cup he had carved out of a piece of wood 나무를 깎아만든 컵, out of는 재료를 나타낸다
lest (접) ~하지 않게(= in order that ~not), 부정의 뜻이기 때문에 anyone이 쓰였다

If water is not supplied quickly to someone who has sweated a lot or hasn't drunk water for a long time, bodily function deteriorates alarmingly. The rate of water loss to the decrease of movement ability is about 1 to 10. For a person who weighs 70kgs, if he loses 2% of his weight, or 1400ml of water, his movement ability will drop 20%. Four percent loss will result in 40% decrease in movement ability, nearly half of the normal state.

Sweat contains ions such as potassium, magnesium and ammonia. As ions control muscle and neural activities, a considerable loss of ions from the body results in spasm or stiffening of the muscles. This is why we often see marathoners suffer from leg cramps during a race. If dehydration gets more serious, perspiration drops to prevent further water loss. This in turn results in the lack of ability to control the body temperature, which rises rapidly. This not only causes physical disorders but also insomnia, hallucination and mental disorders. If the body temperature rises above 40~41°C, the person will lose consciousness, and if water is still not supplied, it will finally result in death.

should hear him.

"Even a genius makes mistakes sometimes. We're all human after all."

Inspiration comes amidst hunger and thirst

One step forward, one step back. By evening Binson was troubled again. Water obtained through solar distilling was more than what he had gotten by collecting dew, but it still was not enough to quench his thirst.

What's more, now his stomach was so empty it felt as if the skin of his belly was hugging his back. It was no wonder, since he had starved for two days. But until he could solve his drinking water problem, he could not go in search of food. If he were to roam around in this heat, he

---

deteriorate (동) 악화시키다, 저하시키다(↔ ameliorate).
potassium (명) 칼륨
spasm 경련
cramp 경련, 쥐. leg cramps = cramps in the leg
insomnia (명) 불면증
hallucination (명) 환각
hug (동) 껴안다→배가 등을 껴안다→뱃가죽이 달라붙다
roam around (정처없이) 돌아다니다, 거닐다

result in 명사 ~라는 결과를 가져오다(=end in)
The rate of water loss to the decrease of movement ability 운동능력저하에 대한 수분손실의 비율
which rises rapidly which = body temperature, 관계절의 계속적 용법이다. '체온이 급격히 상승한다.'
One step forward, one step back 일진일퇴, 일희일비

would surely die of thirst rather than hunger.

Splash, splash, roar. The sound of the waves lingered around Binson's ears. If only he could turn all that sea water into drinking water. He looked at the sea woefully.

"Sea water! It's so useless."

The only way to turn sea water into drinking water is to distill it. But in order to do that, Binson needed fire. Fire was the key in solving both his thirst and hunger. Binson looked down at the blisters he got trying to make a fire and sighed deeply.

"Binson, you are useless."

Water! Fire! Water! Fire! Which is more important? Binson tore at his hair. Who knew that he, at age twenty, would end up on an uninhabited island and worry about these things?

Binson took off his glasses. He hoped he might get a new idea as he did about the solar distiller.

"Hey glasses, tell me when I ask you nicely. How can I make a fire? If you don't answer in one minute, I will break you to pieces."

Fifty-nine seconds later, Binson started kissing his glasses, shouting madly. Then he smiled contentedly and put his glasses back on. His glasses couldn't have really spoken; what could it be that had occurred to him?

"Magnifying glass! That was it. Hahahaha. I'm going to live!"

Of course, you can easily make a fire with a magnifying glass. Unfortunately for Binson, his glasses were not that kind. They were plain glasses - just fashion accessories. Now what?

"Alas! Why didn't I think of this earlier?"

Binson elaborately untied the pack on his waist. Then he took out the camera his mother had given him as a present when he had been admitted to college. The camera lens! That was what Binson had thought about while staring at his glasses.

Happy that he had finally found a way to make a fire, he went to sleep.

'Tomorrow when the sun comes up I will become the great Prometheus of the twenty-first century. I will run out to the shore as soon as I build a fire and make drinking water and cook some clams.'

---

linger (동) 맴돌다, 꾸물대다
blister (명) 물집
Magnifying glass 돋보기
die of 죽다. 병 · 굶주림 · 노령에는 of, 부상 등에는 from 을 쓴다
If only 오직 ~하기만 하면(좋으련만)(= I do wish)

Which is more important (of the two, fire or water)?
Who knew 누가 알았을까? → 아무도 몰랐다 (수사의문문)
Happy that he had finally found a way to make a fire → He was happy to find a way ~형용사 happy 뒤에 오는 부정사는 언제나 원인이라 생각해도 좋다

Then he looked at the sky and mumbled in a worried voice.

"Surely it won't rain tomorrow, will it?"

Binson makes a fire with a strip of film and a lens

Fortunately, it did not rain. The sand was twinkling under the bright sun. Binson first gathered plenty of dry grass and twigs. Then he carefully separated the lens from the body of the camera. He decided to use foreign bills he had exchanged at the airport as carbon paper. It was not as if he was going to need any money on this island.

Binson's eyes shone, too, as the lens twinkled in the sun. He looked inside the camera. It had a big hole where the lens used to be. There he saw the roll of film he had put in at the airport.

"Right. Since film is black it will catch fire better than a bill. I shouldn't be wasting foreign currency in economically hard times like this."

Moved by his own patriotism, Binson put the bill back into his wallet. He then took the film and lens and went out into the bright sunlight.

Haha. Soon I am going to witness the historic moment where a lens becomes a microwave oven.'

The fire made a nice snapping sound.

Moved, Binson stared at the dancing flames. How many times had he seen fire before! Fire at the tip of a cigarette, match fire, fire on the gas range, a bonfire, and even a burning house. But never had the color of the flames seemed so beautiful until now.

As long as he had the lens, he could always make another fire. But Binson decided he would never let this one die. He felt the fire was his hope. Someday he would get out of this island and go back to his beloved family.

My hope will go on as long as this fire stays lit.'

After he had put on some firewood, he suddenly felt drowsy. He had twitched and turned all night, thinking of making a fire. With the sound of burning wood as lullaby, Binson fell into a deep sleep, even forgetting

---

strip (명) 길쭉한 조각, a strip of film → 필름
snap (동) 날카로운 소리를 내다 → 동사가 형용사적으로 쓰인 예
drowsy (형) 나른한, feel ~졸리다
twitch (동) 실룩 움직이다
lullaby (명) 자장가(= cradlesong)
Fortunately, it did not rain = It is fortunate that it didn't rain

foreign currency 외국통화(외화)
(Being) Moved by his own patriotism 자신의 애국심에 뭉클한 감동을 느끼며
never had the color of the flames seemed so beautiful 부사(never) 앞에 위치해 주어·동사가 도치된 형태 → the color of the flame never had seemed~
this one = this fire
get out of '장소에서' 나가다, 떠나다

the fact that he was very hungry.

Robinson Crusoe pays another visit

"Hi Binson! How are you holding up?"

Robinson approached with a cheeky smile on his face. Two rabbits were hanging at his waist, seemingly caught by a trap. They looked at Binson woefully.

He must be eating well, look at his oily face.'

Binson glared at him and snapped,

"Why are you here again?"

"Why, you ask? To remedy your stupidity of course."

"Stupidity? I made a water filter, a distiller and even a fire with a lens."

"Bah! That is nothing to brag about."

Robinson interrupted with a look of pity on his face.

"If you thought of the lens, why didn't you think of the vinyl?"

"What's vinyl got to do with the lens?"

"Thickhead, Listen carefully. On an uninhabited island like this, you have to make do with what you've got. If you put water in a transparent plastic bag you can make a convex lens.

You had a plastic bag and a vinyl raincoat and still couldn't do anything straight for days. Can you still say you're going to succeed as a crash survivor?"

"……."

"Well then, good luck. I'm leaving."

"Wait a second."

"What now? I'm busy. It's time for my snack."

"Just why are you telling me these things after, and not before?"

"It's more fun this way."

"……."

Robinson disappeared into the fog, with the two rabbits hanging at his waist. Binson glared at the back of his head and muttered farewell through clenched teeth.

"I'll see you later."

---

hold up (어떤 상태를) 지속하다, 견디다
brag (동) 자랑하다(= boast)
Thickhead (명) 머리가 둔한 사람, 멍청이
mutter (동) 중얼거리다
make do with~ ~을 최대한 활용하다

convex lens 볼록렌즈, cf) 오목 렌즈 a concave lens
It's time for my snack = it's time for me to have a snack
with the two rabbits hanging at his waist 양태의 부사구로 이때 with는 생략될 수 있다

Aristotle's wisdom revived

Binson ran to the shore as soon as he woke up.

He took the tin can that was lying on the beach and filled it about two-thirds with sea water. If he succeeded in distilling sea water, the whole sea would become his personal, gigantic water tank.

Binson thought hard about how he would make the water distiller.

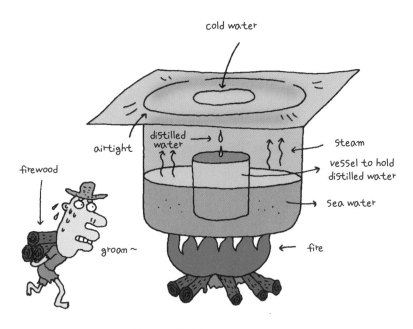

<How to distill seawater>

The principle was simple, but simply boiling water was not going to solve anything. The steam had to be turned to water again, and Binson also needed something to collect the water in one place.

First he cut bamboo and made a tube. He put the bamboo tube in the middle of the tin and adjusted the height of the tube to the tin. Then he covered the tin with the plastic bag. Then he poured some cold water on top of the plastic bag. Now everything was ready. Binson dug out the dirt from under the tin and made a fire.

The sea water began to boil. The plastic bag clouded up with steam. A while later, water drops formed inside the plastic bag, then fell down the bamboo tube. The hot steam was cooled by the cold water on top of the plastic bag to become water again. Binson's idea had worked once again.

Binson emptied the tube and poured more water in the tin can several times. Now he no longer needed to worry about drinking water again. Gulping the salt-free water, he muttered with a grin.

---

grin (명) (이를 드러낸) 웃음. with a ~(이를 드러내어) 싱글벙글 웃으며
two thirds (of the tin)
succeed in~ (~에) 성공하다

adjust A to B A를 B에 맞추다, 조절하다
cloud up 흐려지다
clouded up with steam 수증기로 흐려지다
salt-free 소금기가 없는

Island Rule of Conduct in
order to minimize dehydration

(1) Do not move unnecessarily and sweat. Think that each drop of sweat shortens your life by one minute.

(2) Avoid direct sunlight. Sunbathing in this case is suicide.

(3) Eat as little as possible. Digestion requires a lot of water. (Going on a diet on a deserted island is not for beauty reasons.)

(4) Close your mouth and breathe with your nose. You will lose less moisture. (A person who sleeps with his/her mouth open will die sooner.(Practice while you can.)

(5) Do not lie on the ground when the temperature is hot. The ground temperature may be up to 15°C higher than the atmosphere.

(6) Do not bare your skin to the wind or sun. Always keep your clothes on even if it's hot. This prevents loss of moisture.

(7) If you feel thirsty, drink water until you feel replenished. This will keep you in good physical condition.

(8) Rest in the shade during the day and move at night or dawn. (If you are a nocturnal person, you're in luck.)

"I learned when I was young at the public bath that when steam reaches the cold ceiling, it turns into water. I must have been a genius then, too."

Binson closed his eyes and thought of his youth. To be more exact, he thought of the inside of the public bath. As a small child, he had often followed his mother to the public bath when his father was too busy to take him. But unfortunately, he could not remember anything about the women's side. He opened his eyes and said to himself regretfully,

"I'm smart but have a bad memory, I guess."

2

North star! This is the northern hemisphere

The clams tasted fantastic. He wished there were some hot sauce and some soju, but compared to the last three days he suffered from thirst and hunger, this was truly a king's meal.

'The sea is indeed the source of life."

After his first meal on the island, Binson lay down by the fire, burping

---

North Star 북극성 cf) 남극성 the south pole star
burp (동) 트림하다
clam (명) 조개
the northern hemisphere 북반구

compared to ~에 비교할 때
the last three days (when) he suffered from thirst and hunger 관계부사 when이 생략

loudly.

He looked at the night sky. Countless stars twinkled like gold dust.

For Binson who had been born and raised in Seoul, it was his first time to see such a grand sight. Forgetting his situation for a while, he looked at the stars in wonder and started to look for constellations.

"That's the Big Dipper, that's Cassiopeia and."

You can easily find the North Star once you find the Big Dipper and

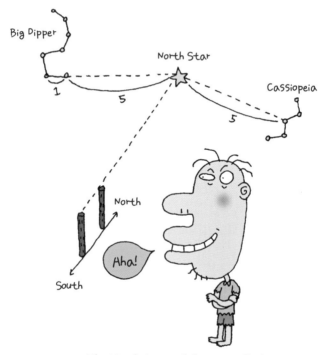

<The North Star and the constellations>

Cassiopeia. The North Star is in the middle of the two constellations.

It showed true north to travelers and seafarers because it conforms to the earth's rotation axis. Pleased to have found the North Star that he had once seen in his youth, he murmured quietly.

"That must be north······ Then this must be the northern hemisphere, because I can see the North Star."

If I keep walking following that star I will reach the North Pole. It might be better than this deserted island. The Eskimos might even roast some penguin meat for me, who knows······'

Binson looked up at the night sky with these idle thoughts. But he was forgetting one important thing. The North Star not only tells you that you are in the Northern Hemisphere, it also tells you the latitude of where you are.

The reason is simple. If Binson were at the North Pole, the North Star would be at the top of his head. If he were near the Equator, it would then

---

constellation (명) 별자리
Big Dipper 북두칠성 cf. Little Dipper 작은곰자리의 소북
  두칠성
once (접) 일단 ~하면
true north 정북(正北)
latitude (명) 위도

Equator (명) 적도
gold dust 금가루
conform to~ ~과 일치하다
keep walking following that star ~저 별을 따라서 계속
  걷다

<The location of the North Star and latitude>

be near the horizon. The latitude of the Equator is 0° and that of the North Pole is 90°. Therefore, the angle of the North Star and the ground becomes the latitude of where Binson is now.

Of course, there is some error. The Earth is oval in shape, and if you draw a vertical line from the ground, the line does not cross the center of the earth. The maximum difference between the vertical line from the ground and the line that meets the center of the earth is 11.5°. In other words, if the North Star is right at a 90° location, that point won't be the North Pole.

North Star,
the beacon in the night sky

All celestial bodies move with time except the North Star. This is because the North Star is located north of the earth's rotation axis. Its distance from Earth is about 800 light years. If you can see the North Star in the night, it means you are in the northern hemisphere.

It is commonly thought that the North Star is the brightest among the stars, but it is not true. There are countless stars much brighter than the North Star.

Hipparchos, the Greek astronomer of 2,000 years ago drew up the catalogue of the stars, dividing them into 6 magnitudes according to its brightness. A 1st magnitude star was the brightest, and a 6th magnitude star the dimmest. Each step in magnitude differs by a factor of about 2.5. An m=6 star is only one hundredth in brightness compared to an m=1 star. A star brighter than m=1 is m=0, and if brighter than m=0, it is expressed in negative (-).

According to this method the North Star is only m=2.1 in brightness. There are three stars brighter than m=0, and 21 stars of m=0 or brighter. There are more than 40 m=2 stars, or brighter than the North Star. The brightest star visible in the northern hemisphere is Sirius, the alpha star in the constellation Canis Major.

However, supposing the stars are all at a same distance from the earth, the 'absolute magnitude' changes. From earth, the sun (150million kilometers from Earth) is m=-26.8, and the North Star m=2.1. But the absolute magnitude of the sun is 4.8 and North Star is -3.7. If we look at the brightness itself, the North Star is two thousand times brighter than the sun.

The North Star won't last forever. Like a rotating toy top, the earth's rotation axis makes a circular movement, which is called precession. It takes about 25800 years for the axis to make a full circle. During that time the axis moves slightly, thus the location of the North Star changes slowly.

Even now the North Star is about 50′ (minutes) away from the earth's rotation axis, and as time passes we will have to look for another star to replace the North Star. According to astronomers' calculations, in 6000 years the alpha star of the Cepheus will be the new lodestar, and in 12000 years the alpha star of Lyra (Vega) will take its place. Once a marine is always a marine, but not for the North Star.

You cannot see the North Star in the southern hemisphere. Not that there is any particular reason, except that Earth is not transparent. There, the Southern Cross (Crux) is used in determining one's bearings.

Even so, there is no problem in roughly guessing the current location.

Binson had been too excited at the grand scenery and overlooked a key factor in determining where he was. But then, even if he did know where he was, it wouldn't make much of a difference.

The maximum difference 최대오차
beacon (명) (높은 곳에 있는) 신호, 봉화
celestial body 천체
magnitude (명) (별의) 광도, 등급. a star of the first = 1 등성
supposing (접) ~라고 가정하면, 만약 ~이라면(= if) *that이 없는 것에 주의할 것
toy top 장난감 팽이
precession (명) 세차(歲差) 운동
lodestar (명) 길잡이 별. the ~북극성(= polestar).
bearing (명) 방위
that of the North Pole에서 that = The latitude

It commonly thought that~ 흔히 ~라 생각한다 = They commonly think that~
by a factor of about 2.5에서 by는 '만큼' 이란 뜻이다
According to ~에 따르면
It takes about 25800 years for the axis to make ~ 에서처럼 It takes 시간 표현 + to V은 '~만큼의 시간이 걸린다' 는 뜻이다
in 6000 years 6000년 후에, 미래와 함께 쓰인 in은 '~후에 라는 뜻
Even so 그렇기는 하나, 그렇다 하더라도
make much of ~소중히 하다, 중시하다

The third night on the island wore on, but Binson could not sleep. As his immediate worries about water and fire were solved, other problems dawned upon him.

"What am I going to eat? I can't eat clam everyday. Just how long am I going to have to stay here? I hope I'm not going to spend all my good years here. Is there a way to get out of here?"

First he had to send a distress signal. How could he do this where there was no means of communication? The first thing to come to mind was fire. If he made a fire in various locations of the island, a passing ship or plane may spot them.

Strike when the iron is hot, they say.'

Binson immediately went out to the beach and made a bonfire and put plenty of firewood on it, praying all the while that someone would see this.

'At night even a cigarette light is visible from far away. A fire this big is bound to be seen.'

But he was soon disappointed. He realized that no ship or plane had passed in the last three days.

"I will have to look around the island tomorrow. There may be a ship that passes at the opposite side."

The second method was writing SOS. He would write the letters on the wide beach. It would be visible from a plane, even if Binson was not.

Surely the pilot will be able to read it.'

Binson woke from his light sleep and went out to the beach with daybreak. Then he wrote SOS on the beach, as big as he could. This was the common language of all crash victims. Just writing the word made him confident he will get rescued soon, and his spirits lightened up. He did not forget to write the word as far from the sea as possible, lest the tide may wash it away.

Suddenly another problem struck him. Writing on the sand will disappear if it rains. It had never rained since he had woken up on the island, but he could never be sure. The hot humid weather was sure sign of rain to come in the near future.

"I'll have to look for another way."

---

wore on (시간이) 천천히 지나가다. 여기에서 on은 진행의 뜻이다
dawned upon ~에게 나타나다
a way to get out of here 여기에서 탈출할 방법
a distress signal 조난신호 → 구조신호
plenty of firewood 많은 장작. plenty of는 수와 양 모두와 쓰인다

is bound to = be obliged to 꼭 ~하다, ~해야 할 운명이다
the opposite side 반대편
SOS 문자 자체로는 아무런 의미도 없다. save our souls[ship]의 약자라고 하는 것은 속설
with daybreak 동이 트기 무섭게 cf) at ~새벽에
as big as he could = as big as possible 가능한한 크게

Binson's answer for the rainy season was rocks. If he wrote the word with rocks it would not wash away so easily.

'The stones of the Incas make an intricate drawing when you look from the sky.'

In the midst of collecting stones on the beach, a sudden thought struck him. He was experiencing first hand the beginnings of human civilization, in the 21st century.

Let's go! Exploring the island

After he finished writing SOS with rocks Binson gathered as much clams as he could. It was going to be his source of nutrition during his exploration. Unless he found some fruits, clam was going to be the only food for him.

After he had had his fill of roasted clams as breakfast, he put the

---

intricate (형) 복잡한, 난해한
when you look from the sky 하늘에서 내려다볼 때
In the midst of ~속에, *사람과 쓰일 때는 in one's
  midst : in our midst 우리 중에

source of nutrition 영양원
his fill 충분함, 가득함, → had had his fill of roasted clams
  구운 조개를 실컷 먹다

remaining clam in the plastic bag. Then he put his other belongings in the sack he wore at the waist.

He did not know whether he would come back or settle in another spot. He could find a much better place than here, with fresh water flowing and fruits hanging on the trees. If he could see boats passing by, all the better.

"First I'll climb up to a high spot and check out the geographical layout of the whole island. Mother used to say if the housing lot is good, everything will be fine······ If I had known better, I would have learned geomantics(Feng Suei)."

As he was about to leave he felt as if he was going to miss this place.

'After all it was my home for the last few days······.'

Traces of bonfire, heaps of shells sitting on the ashes, and the little piece of Incan civilization he had made with rocks······ A grin came to his face looking at the site.

"Haha. Some day someone might come here and say they found the housing site and shell mound of a primitive man. Maybe I should have made a dolmen while I was at it."

Binson hung two plastic bags filled with drinking water at both sides of his waist, picked up a burning stick from the bonfire, and set out on his exploration of the island.

The reason he brought the torch with him was not just that he would not let the fire die. It could protect him in case he met a wild beast, and if a plane happened to pass by, it could be the moving distress signal.

Let's go! As Binson started out on his grand enterprise a small hope lingered in his heart.

"This island may not be deserted after all. If there are no civilians, there could at least be a troop of soldiers dispatched here, like Dokdo Island. It doesn't matter what nationality they are, just let there be someone!"

The mountain was much more rugged than he had expected. It was also covered with a thick forest. Binson had already been struggling for hours. There wasn't a trail he could follow, which made it even more difficult. Binson, whose only experience at mountain climbing was going hiking near Seoul, was now climbing a virgin peak that even Hoe Young-ho had not climbed.

At last he reached the summit. A wide view of the island came to his sight. The island was oval in shape and was surrounded by the vast sea. He could not find a trace of land in any direction. He realized once again that he was alone in this lonely island in the far seas.

"Does this mean I can't get out of here unless someone finds me······?"

But he had no time to despair. He had to find somewhere to stay so that someone could find him later. Somewhere easily viewable, somewhere that would shelter him from the rain and wild beasts, somewhere he could easily find water and food. He squinted his eyes and thoroughly examined the island.

Suddenly Binson's eyes flashed. He could see a vast tidal flat along the shore. Behind the flat was a low hill and thick forest at the back of the hill. Binson nodded, murmuring softly.

"If there is a tidal flat, it means there is also a river or stream. The forest will give me plenty of firewood, some fruits and vegetables. The hill will be a good spot to look for ships passing by.

It would also be better for avoiding flood or storm. "Alright. Let's go there."

The sun was already setting and Binson hurried down the mountain. Halfway downhill he stopped to look down at his new nest. The sun was hanging on the horizon and everything around him was colored red by the sunset.

'Hmmm. The view is excellent too. I sure picked a nice spot······."

He could almost hear his mother's voice.

"Do you know why your father always used to go bankrupt? It was because the house was on a bad site. Look. Now that we have moved to this new house, everything is going well. Our ancestors didn't look for

---

rugged (형) 험준한, 바위투성이의
trail (명) 산길
squint (동) 눈을 가늘게 뜨고 보다
thoroughly (부) 철저하게 (= completely)
Halfway (부) 중간쯤에 Halfway downhill → 산 중턱에서
a virgin peak 처녀봉

came to his sight 시야에 들어오다
in any direction 어떤 방향으로나
tidal flat 조수로 생긴 편평한 땅 →갯벌
The hill will be a good spot to look for ships passing by에서 보는 주체가 없다. 주체를 써놓고 싶으면 부정사로 동사 앞에 for Nobinson to look for~
Now that ~이니까, ~이므로(=because, as)

propitious sites for no reason······ Binson! What's that look on your face? You want to get grounded?"

Binson gets lost

"Jesus! Which way should I go?"

Binson moaned continuously. It must have been at least three or four hours since he got lost. From the peak the hill had seemed to be about a two hours' walk at the most, and now he could not find it anywhere. He had walked in the direction he guessed at and had entered a thick forest. Now he could not tell where he was or where he was going.

What's more now that the sun had set he was surrounded in total darkness. He was carrying a torch but he could only see a few steps ahead. His careful steps slowed him down, and he was dead tired from walking with his nerves on end lest he should meet a wild beast.

"Damn this island. If there is no street light, there should at least be some road signs······."

Finally Binson gave up on walking. It was meaningless to keep on going when he could not tell which direction he was going. Since he could end up going in the wrong direction, he decided it would be better to wait until daybreak.

But then again, even when the sun did come up, his chances of

---

propitious (형) 형편 좋은 propitious sites 길지(吉地)
ground (동) 좌초시키다, 땅에 던지다 get grounded 땅에 엎어지다 → 두들겨 맞다
moan (동) 신음소리를 내다, 끙끙거리다
tell (동) 말하다 → 구분하다
lest (접) ~하지 않게(= in order that ·· not), 시제로 보통

미국에서는 가정법 현재, 영국에서는 should를 쓴다
meaningless (형) 의미가 없는
got lost 방향감각을 상실하다, 길을 잃다 = lose the way
at the most 많아야, 기껏해야
walking with his nerves on end 신경을 곤두세우고 걷다
end up ~ing 결국 ~하게 되다

finding the right direction were slim. He probably wouldn't be able to see the hill and tidal flat from the low ground. He would have to go back up the mountain to make sure, and then the sun might set again. It would take the same amount of time it did yesterday, unless the mountain had somehow shrunk overnight.

If he had something to chop a tree with, he could guess the direction by looking at the annual ring. The side where the space between the rings is wider is south. But it was impossible to cut a tree with the pocket knife he had. A pencil maybe, a tree, no.

"Hmmm, spitting to decide the direction won't help either······."

After thinking for a long time, his eyes flashed again. He had remembered the sunset he had seen while coming downhill.

"That direction was west, because the sun set in that direction. So all I have to do is see where the sun comes up in the morning and walk the opposite way. I'll wake up as early as possible and wait for the sunrise."

Having made up his mind he made bonfires on several ground dugouts, so that the fire wouldn't spread. Then he gathered some leaves and covered it with his raincoat. He used to be a late sleeper but tomorrow he had to wake up early no matter what. Another thought came to his mind as he tried to get some sleep.

"When I woke up early once in a while, mother always used to say 'the sun must have risen from the west this morning' ······If I wake up early tomorrow, which way is the sun going to come up any way?"

Telling the direction with a stick

The sun rose. Binson decided to believe the direction the sun had risen was east, despite his mother's words. Then he started to walk straight in the opposite direction.

'I should be able to reach the west shore by sunset at the latest······.'

But soon Binson realized what an unreliable way it had been. Unless he was walking on a boulevard, it was almost impossible to tell the direction on such a winding way blocked by hills and trees. After he had passed a thick strip of trees, he lost his sense of direction again.

Of course if he waited for sunset he would be able to find west again.

---

shrink (동) 줄어들다
chop (동) 자르다, 쓰러뜨리다
dugout (명) 대피호
strip (명) 길쭉한 조각, 길 → a thick strip of trees 숲
annual ring 나이테

make up one's mind 결심하다, 마음의 결정을 내리다
used to V ~하곤 했다(과거의 습관을 나타내는 조동사 used to)
no matter what 무슨 일이 있더라도 → 반드시
at the latest 늦어도(the가 없어도 된다 → at latest)

But then it would get dark soon and he would get lost yet again. He glanced at the sun but it was useless. It is hard to tell the direction by looking at the sun except at sunrise and sunset.

"This means trouble. I can't go back up the mountain now······."

Binson dropped his head feeling distrait. His shadow hung on the steamy ground.

'Poor shadow is going through a tough time because of its master······'

Suddenly Binson's eyes lit up.

"Shadow! I can use the shadow. Hahahaha. That's it!"

Indeed, that was it. The shadow is the only trace that indicates the exact movement of the sun. Binson's brain was being upgraded at ultra high speed ever since he got to this island.

Binson found a straight stick and stuck it on the ground. Then he drew a straight line from the tip of the stick's shadow to where the stick was on the ground. Then he marked the length of the shadow every twenty minutes, using his wristwatch. The shadow became shorter then suddenly started to get longer again. It had now become afternoon.

Half a day had passed. There were short and long lines around the

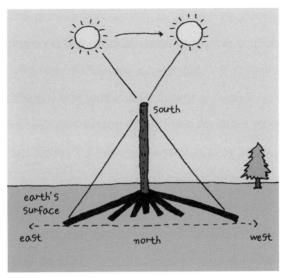

<Finding the direction with a stick's shadow>

stick. Binson picked out the lines that were about the same length and measured their length using his fingers. Soon, he found two lines that were exactly the same length. Binson sprang to his feet.

"I found it! Yeah!"

distrait (형) 망연한, 멍한
steamy (형) 김이 자욱한
tip (명) 끝, 꼭대기 * the tip of the sticks 막대기의 끝
get dark 어두워지다
glanced at 흘끗 보다
It is hard to V = it is difficult to V ~하기는 어렵다

go through (괴로움 등을) 경험하다, 겪다
every twenty minutes 매 20분 → 20분마다
It had now become afternoon 벌써 오후가 되다 * 비인칭 it
Half a day 하루의 절반, 반나절
sprang to his feet 벌떡 일어서다

The principles are simple. If you stand a stick on the ground, two identical shadows form, once in the morning and once in the afternoon. When the length of the shadows are identical, it means the sun is at the exact opposite at those moments. Therefore if you connect the tip of the two shadows by a straight line it shows true west and true east.

Then which is west and which is east? Of course the shadow that formed in the morning points west and the shadow in the afternoon points east, because a shadow always forms on the opposite side of the sun. When the sun moves from east to west, the shadow moves in the opposite direction-from west to east. If you draw a vertical line from the line that points east and west, you now also know north and south.

Having found the direction, Binson triumphantly walked west. This time he picked a tree far away as a signpost so he would not get lost again.

"Wait, here I come. Nobinson is coming!"

His gait became faster.

If only I had a magnet

The way to the new home was far and rough. He had hurried his way, changing signposts several times, but still the hill he was headed to didn't come to sight. It became dark again, and finally Binson sank to the ground moaning.

He looked up at the sky. If he could see the North Star he was going to guess the direction somehow. But the stars that shone so brightly last night were nowhere to be seen tonight. The sky was covered with clouds.

"What am I going to do? Am I going to have to wait until daybreak again?"

Binson glanced at his watch. Then he rapped himself on the head, scolding himself.

"You idiot. This isn't home. What use is it to look at a watch when the time isn't even correct? You think the watch is a compass?"

signpost (명) 지표, 단서
gait (명) 걸음걸이, 발걸음
scold (동) 꾸짖다, 비난하다 * scold oneself 자책하다
the exact opposite 정반대 → the opposite side of the sun 태양의 반대편
the line that points east and west 동쪽과 서쪽을 가리

키는 선 → 동서를 잇는 선
a tree far away 멀리 있는 나무
sank to the ground 땅바닥에 주저앉다
was covered with ~로 덮이다
rapped himself on the head 그의 머리를 때리다 *신체의 일부이기 때문에 정관사 the를 사용

The earth is a gigantic magnet. Scientists believe that the large liquid core within the Earth generates a magnetic field. The origin of the Earth's magnetic field is not yet completely understood, but is thought to be associated with electrical currents produced by the coupling of convective effects and rotation in the spinning liquid outer core made of iron and nickel.

A magnetic compass works based on the 'opposites attract' rule of magnets. The Earth's South end is at the North Pole and the North end is at the South Pole. The North end of the compass' needle is attracted to the Earth's South end to point North, and the South end of the needle is attracted to the Earth's North end to point South.

The geographical north is called 'true north' and the direction the needle of the compass points to is called 'magnetic north.' True north and magnetic north do not coincide with each other. In other words, if you follow north on your compass you won't reach the North Pole.

This is because magnetic north changes slightly according to changes in the Earth's magnetic field. Currently the declination of the Earth's north-south axis and that of the compass is about 11.5°. If

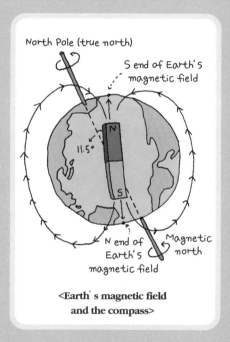

North Pole (true north)

S end of Earth's magnetic field

N

S

11.5°

N end of Earth's magnetic field

Magnetic north

<Earth's magnetic field and the compass>

you were to head out for the North Pole depending solely on your compass you would end up somewhere near Hudson Bay in northern Canada, some 1,800 kilometers away from the North Pole. All the while complaining the compass is broken. If you were to head out for the South Pole you would end up somewhere in the ocean south of Australia.

The changes in magnetic north can also be found in records. In 1580 the compass needle of London skewed 11° east from true north, and in 1660 it coincided with true north. In 1820 and 1970 it skewed 24° and 7° northwest, respectively. It is suspected that a small whirl formed in the midst of the large convection movement in the outer core was the cause of this. Observations show that even now magnetic north changes by about 0.1° every year.

If only the wristwatch was a compass. But that was just wishful thinking. If all his wishes could come true he wished that his arms would become wings and the sea would become land so that he could escape from the island. What's important when stranded on an uninhabited island is not equipment in themselves but the ability to make your own equipment. If you can make them you will use them, if you can't make them, you will not. Binson knew this already from the last few days on the island.

Tick-tack tick-tack. The needle turned. The useless thing that could not tell him time nor direction. But then on a deserted island, nothing is useless. Binson murmured, looking down at his watch. It was the monologue of a true island man.

"Is there a way to turn this watch into a compass?"

On the starless night, Binson's eyes began to twinkle.

"Was it in Earth Science class that I learned this? The biggest magnet on Earth is Earth itself. And the reason the needle of the compass points north is because of the magnetic field formed in the Earth's core······."

Correct. The reason the compass can tell directions is because Earth's magnetic field attracts the compass needle. All magnets are destined to point toward its opposite end.

This is the instinctive longing between the North end and South end.

"The magnet is the problem. If I had a magnet I could make the second hand of the watch into a compass needle."

Correct again. When a metal touches a magnet it magnetizes briefly. This is why a piece of metal that touches a magnet pulls another piece of metal.

"If someone would lend me a magnet for a minute I could make a compass······."

Incorrect. You cannot make a compass just by touching the second hand of the watch to a magnet. The North and South ends have to be formed at the same time. In order to do this, you can rub the needle from

---

devotion (명) 헌신, 일편단심
magnet (명) 자석
magnetic field 자기장(磁氣場)
convective (형) 대류적인
declination (명) 편차, 기울기
whirl (명) 소용돌이
convection (명) 대류 →convection movement 대류운동
attract (동) 끌어당기다
instinctive (형) 본능적인
magnetize 자성을 갖다
coincide with each other 서로 일치하다 * coincide with
   ~이기 때문에 each other 앞에 with가 쓰인다
that of the compass에서 that = axis
depending solely on your compass 나침반에만 의존

한 채
It is suspected that~ ~으로 추정되다(=one guesses
   that~)
If only ~한다면 좋을텐데 가정의 강조로 I do wish that~
What's important when stranded on an
uninhabited island가 동사 is의 주어
Was it in Earth Science class that I learned this?
   강조용법이 의문문으로 된 것
are destined to V ~할 운명이다 = be obliged to V
I could make the second hand of the watch into a
compass needle 시계의 초침을 나침반 바늘로 만들다
   (→바꾸다)
This is why~ 그것이 ~하는 이유이다 → '그래서' 라고 해
   석하면 간단하다

one end of the magnet to the other. This way you can transfer the magnetic force of the magnet into the needle.

"What use would it be to make a compass needle with the watch? I can't put it on my palm. Neither can the needle float in the air······. Ah yes. I can put in on a leaf and float it on water."

Correct again. If you put the compass needle on top of your palm the friction caused by the uneven and coarse surface would hinder the movement of the needle. But if you were to put it on a leaf and float it on still water it would be almost frictionless and you will be able to find directions.

Our smart Binson got three out of four answers correct. But what use could it be. Everything was possible only if he had a magnet. Unless of course he could find a piece of natural magnet right then and there, Binson could not make a compass even with the perfect plan.

Night wore on. Binson's sighs became deeper too. As hard as he thought, he could not figure out a way to make a magnet. Binson had caught up with Prometheus and Aristotle, but there was nothing he could do about this problem.

"Oh-oh! If I had just a little piece of magnet······."

Binson's deep sigh spread into the deep of the night. The next day he would have to find his way by using the stick again.

Like the frontiersman of the West

The sun was already high when Binson woke up. He had practically passed out as soon as he reached the hill at dawn and had slept until now. Days of walking had left him with aching legs and sore feet. Because he hadn't eaten since he ran out of the clam he brought, his stomach was sending urgent rescue signals again.

The site he had picked out was indeed a perfect spot. Since there were no high mountains around the hill he had a clear view of the sea. Toward the sea there was a water flow which was small to call a river but wider than a stream. In the water he could see some big fish. The tidal flat made

float (동) 띄우다, 뜨게 하다
friction (명) 마찰
uneven (형) 편평하지 않은, 울퉁불퉁한
hinder (동) 방해하다 * 명사형: hindrance
still (형) 잔잔한, 움직이지 않는
spread (동) 퍼지다(into)
aching (형) 아픈, 쑤시는 ← ache (동) 아프다, 쑤시다
got three out of four answers correct 5형식 문장, 네

문제 중 세 개를 맞추다
what use could it be 무슨 소용인가? = what is the
  use of getting three out of four~
Night wore on. Binsons sighs became deeper too
  wear on과 become deeper는 결국 같은 뜻이다
figure out 생각해내다
caught up with ~을 따라잡다
ran out of~ ~을 다 써버리다, 동나다

of sand and mud was full of shellfish he didn't even know the names of.

"When I build a house here, at least I won't have to worry about food and water."

Binson slowly walked along the shore gathering shellfish. After he had eaten some, he planned to go into the woods and find some food.

'I will pick fruit, catch some fish and set some snares to catch small animals.'

His mouth watered as he remembered the rabbits that were hanging at Robinson's waist. He could hardly remember the last time he had feasted on some juicy sizzling meat.

Food wasn't the only thing he needed immediately. The thick clouds that were forming since yesterday did not look good. If this kind of weather continued the rainy season was sure to come soon. If it starts to rain finding shelter would become a big problem, let alone hunting. He had to find a safe shelter before that.

'First I will build the frame with wood. Then I will paste it with mud from the tidal flat to make walls and cover the roof with layers of leaves. I almost forgot. I will first have to do some foundation work with rocks to prevent flooding. When I catch some animals I will be able to make a bed with the skin. What about the toilet? Should I just go anywhere?'

Was it because he had arrived after so much hardship? Or was it because of the principle of feng suei his mother had told him about? Binson's heart swelled with hope about his new life in his new home. With his lips closed firmly Binson looked at the sea and muttered as if pledging himself.

"I can get out. Until then I will live a good life, just like the pioneers of the West."

oh no! Binson misses the ship

After Binson finished his meal, he made a fire on top of the hill as a distress signal. Then he went down to the beach and wrote SOS with rocks.

---

shellfish (명) 갑각류의 동물 → 조개
snare (명) 덫
sizzling (동) 지글지글 소리를 내는 ← sizzle(동)
layer (명) 겹, 층
hardship (명) 고난, 역경
swell (동) 부풀다
pledge (동) 맹세하다 pledge oneself 다짐하다
he didnt even know the names of = (which) he

didnt even know the names of에서 of의 목적어로 관계절 생략. 그러나 of which he didnt even know the names에서 생략 불가능
feast on ~을 잔뜩 즐기다
build the frame with wood 나무로 틀을 짜다
paste A with B A에 B를 붙이다
With his lips closed firmly 입술을 굳게 다물고. * 양태의 부사구로 with의 생략이 가능하다

'Shall I write it in Italic or Gothic? I do have a good handwriting······. When I was in high school the reason Malsuk(Binson's girlfriend) came over to me was because of my handwriting in the love letters. How could she not remember anything about the letter except the handwriting?'

At that moment, Binson's eyes lit up like a lamp. He had spotted a small dot glimmering in the distance as he glanced at the horizon.

"What could that be? It seems to be moving······."

Binson bolted to his feet, staring hard at the far sea. Then a cry of joy burst from his mouth. It was a short cry, like the howl of a wild beast.

"A ship!!"

Binson ran to the top of the hill with all his might. He shouted at the top of his lungs, waving his arms. He didn't care if it was a pirate ship or a phantom ship. Please, please find me······.

"Hey, Over here."

But the ship didn't seem to be coming any closer, it just moved further away. Binson's eyes finally caught sight of the fire he had just made.

'I have to make a bigger fire.'

Binson picked leaves and wood around him and threw them into the fire.

"Please look this way. See the fire, or even the smoke······ Please!"

But it was no use. Binson's frantic shouts began to subside. A while later, the ship finally went over the horizon. Binson fell to the ground, dumbfounded.

"It was my chance. It was my golden chance to get out of here······ Ahhhh, am I going to die on this island, never being able to escape?"

Tears ran down his cheeks. His shoulders began to shake ever more fiercely. He could not even cry out with his sore throat. "Croak—" was all that he could mutter.

Binson's silent weep went on. Above the empty sea where the ship had left, a bird was flying in circles innocently.

---

handwriting (명) 필체
spot (동) 찾아내다
howl (명) 울음소리
pirate ship 해적선
phantom ship 유령선
frantic (형) 미친듯한, 광적인
subside (동) 가라앉다, 잦아들다
dumbfound (동) 아연하게 만들다, 얼떨떨하게 하다
weep (명) 울음. silent weep → 소리없는 통곡
glimmering in the distance 멀리에서 깜빡거리는

bolt to his feet 벌떡 일어서다 = spring to his feet
with all his might 있는 힘을 다해서, 힘껏
at the top of his lungs 가슴이 터지도록
He didnt care if it was a pirate ship or a phantom ship 해적선이든 유령선이든 개의치 않았다
it was no use = There's no use (~ing) 소용없는 짓이었다
fell to the ground 땅바닥에 풀썩 주저앉았다
with his sore throat 에서의 with는 '~때문에' 라는 뜻이다

"I was stupid. I was the most stupid person on earth."

Binson blamed himself, with a numb look on his face. There were clear tear marks on his tanned cheeks. He must have sat there all day without a budge. It was growing dark, and the red sun was half submerged in the sea.

"You fool. Don't even think of escaping with that head."

Binson had just realized his mistake. He had realized that during the day, it is much more effective to send up smoke because fire is not easily visible. In order to do that he should have burned wet leaves and wood. He hadn't thought of this simple principle and had thrown dry firewood into the fire. It was no wonder the ship had passed by without spotting him.

"Binson, you good-for-nothing arrowhead. What were you going to do with the lens? Were you saving it to eat later?"

It is far more effective to reflect sunlight with a piece of glass than to make a fire or send up smoke. Binson knew that when seamen were stranded they used mirrors to send out distress signals. But when he did find a ship he had not thought of any of that.

Of course the people on the ship may not have found him even if he had used the lens. But failing after trying and not trying at all are so different. For Binson, what was most regrettable was the fact that he had not tried what he was capable of doing.

Binson sat in self-remorse all day and finally got back up on his feet late into the night. The ship had already passed by. He knew that it was useless to regret what had already passed.

"Yeah. Ships travel on the same course, so another one will come soon. I should prepare for it if I'm not going to miss another one. Sitting here doing nothing is even more foolish."

Binson slowly walked toward the bonfire. He blew on the fire and found a live flicker. It seemed dead yet it was alive inside, and it comforted him.

---

numb (형) 감각을 잃은, 멍한
tanned cheeks 햇살에 그을린 뺨
budge (명) 움직임. without a budge → 꼼짝하지 않고 (=motionlessly)
strand (동) 배가 좌초되다. 수동태로 쓰일 때에는 '오도 가도 못하게 되다'
self-remorse (명) 자책, 자괴
blew ← blow (동) 입김을 불다
flicker (명) 불씨. a live flicker 살아 있는 불씨
Binson had just realized his mistake 과거완료시제로 쓰인 것은 앞의 사건에 대한 설명이기 때문이다.

he should have burned ~should have + pp는 '~했어야 했는데' 라는 뜻으로 과거 행위에 대한 후회를 표현한다
good-for-nothing arrowhead 아무 짝에도 쓸모없는 화살촉 → 바보
may not have found ~하지 못했을 수도 있다. * 조동사 may V의 과거형은 may have + pp이다
late into the night 밤늦게. cf) the late 12th century 12세기 말
another one = another ship

A while later the fire began to crackle again. It was also the sound of Binson's hopes rising again. As the hill enveloped in darkness lit up with the fire, so did Binson' eyes with hope.

crackle (동) 딱딱 소리를 내다
the sound of Binson's hopes rising again에서 of 이

하는 동명사절이다. 이 절에서 Binson's hopes가 동명 사로 사용된 rising의 의미상 주어이다

3

Building a house

Building a house was not as easy as he had first thought. Binson soon realized that the cozy log cabin he had seen in the outskirts of Seoul was not going to happen for him. There were plenty of trees in the forest, but he had nothing to cut them with.

"Maybe I can make a stone axe?"

Binson thought of the comic books with primitives holding stone

---

cozy (형) 안락한, 아늑한
outskirts (명) 변두리, 교외. 거의 언제나 복수로 쓰인다
as he had first thought 생각했던 것만큼(시제의 사용에

주의할 것)
the comic books 만화책

axes. But grinding a stone sharp enough to chop wood was possible only for the skilled technician of the Neolithic era.

And Binson did not have much time. He had to build a house no matter what, before the rain started.

"It would be so cool to have a sawing machine right now."

Binson immediately hit himself on the head and changed his line.

"What good would a sawing machine do when there is no electricity?"

Binson finally had to change his plans of building a top class villa.

Crack, snap. Countless branches were broken. Binson is now walking in the woods gathering branches the size of his arm. Some he broke with sheer strength, some he cling to, and if that didn't work, he went up the tree and stumped on the branch.

Binson's new plan was to build a tent type cabin. He would make a frame shaped like an 'A', fill the holes with mud, and cover it with large leaves like tiles. Then he would have a pretty nice house. He would use vines to tie the twigs together. Fortunately there were plenty of thick vines that Tarzan might have swing on.

After a whole day's hard work, he had enough branches to build a house. Now what he needed were some thick wood to use as pillars. If nothing else, at least the pillars had to be sturdy enough to hold up the entire house.

Looking around, Binson found two small trees about the size of his thighs. Of course he could not break it with sheer strength but he already had a master plan in his head.

"If I can't break it, I'll uproot it."

Uproot a tree with bare hands? Binson was no Hercules. And there wasn't any wild ginseng lying around in the forest.

"If you don't have the muscles, use the brain. Man didn't become lord of all creation by strength."

Binson broke a twig so that one end would be pointed, and started to dig with it. Fortunately the ground was soft enough so that he didn't need a shovel. After five or six times of removing the dirt he had dug up and

---

Neolithic era 신석기 시대
cool (형) 좋은 (= excellent). 주로 구어에서의 의미이다
sheer (형) 순수한, 전적인
stump (동) 쿵쿵거리다
vine (명) 덩굴. 대개는 포도덩굴
pillar (명) 기둥
sturdy (형) 튼튼한
thigh (명) 허벅지
Uproot (동) 뿌리째 뽑다
point (동) 뾰족하게 깎다.
no matter what 반드시, 어떻게 해서라도
It would be so cool to have a sawing machine right

now to V가 가정법의 조건걸로 사용되었다(= If I had a sawing machine right now)
cling to ~에 매달리다
swing on 타고 매달리다, 흔들다
If nothing else 다른 것은 몰라도
the pillars had to be sturdy enough to hold up the entire house 기둥만은 집 전체를 떠받칠 만큼 튼튼해야 한다
the ground was soft enough so that he didnt need a shovel = the ground was too soft for him to need a shovel

digging again, the trees finally began to show their roots that were buried deep in the ground. Moist root with fine root hair on it.

When the roots were almost bare, Binson stood up and pushed the tree. He let out a great yawp.

He felt through his shoulders that the tree was leaning. Sinews stood up on his forehead and arms.

'Fall, fall, fal······.'

A moment later, two figures dropped to the ground simultaneously. One was the tree; the other was Binson hugging the tree.

Finally he was done with lumbering. Two trees and one person lay parallel on the ground. Lying there on the ground exhausted, Binson muttered in awe.

"When I asked mother for an allowance mother always said I was going to root up the pillar. Mother had foresight."

Island villa on the hill

Having uprooted two pillars, Binson immediately went to work on building the cabin.

First he adjusted the height of the two pillars and drove them into the ground 4~5 meters apart, then leaned two thick branches at each pillar diagonally. He tied the top of the pillars with vines and dug the ground to hold the branches firmly in place. At the sides, he tied some long branches into place.

Fixing the pillars on the ground required a lot of care. If the cabin were to blow away in the wind he would end up homeless. Binson treaded the ground to harden it until his feet hurt, but still not satisfied he kicked hard at the pillar.

"Ow! Who fixed this pillar so hard?"

Binson decided to make windows on the sides facing north and south for ventilation. Fortunately he had a transparent sheet of plastic that he could use instead of glass.

After filling the holes between the branches with mud and letting it

---

Sinew (명) 힘줄
lumber (동) 나무를 벌채하다
allowance (명) 용돈
foresight (명) 선견지명
adjust (동) 조절하다, 맞추다
diagonally (부) 대각선으로
tread (동) 밟다, 밟아 다지다
ventilation (명) 환기, 통풍
let out 소리를 지르다(= give out)

was done with ~을 마치다
in awe 경외심에 싸여
Having uprooted two pillars = After he had uprooted two pillars
end up 결국 ~이 되다. * end up homeless 결국 집없는 사람이 되다
still not satisfied he kicked hard at the pillar 만족하지 못해서 기둥을 발로 세게 찼다
so ~ (that) 용법으로 결과절로 해석한다

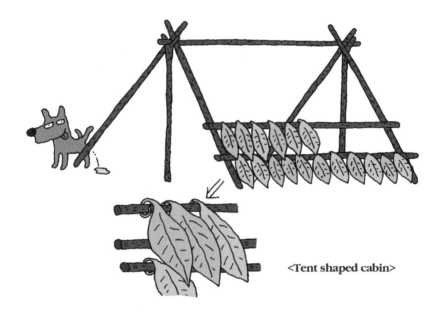

<Tent shaped cabin>

dry in the sun, it will become a nice clay wall. Covering the outside of the wall with large thick leaves would cut off some of the sunlight. On the roof he would overlap the leaves like roof tiles. That way the rain would fall down the sides without leaking into the cabin.

As he was building the frame of the house, Binson suddenly remembered playing with building blocks when he was a kid.

'It only took a couple of hours no matter how big the house was······ Building a real house is so hard, even if it's just a one-room cabin. It's going to take at least a week at this rate.'

84

After a good while the frame of the house was finally complete. Although it was far from the cozy cabin he had first thought of, it was a long way from the nights in the open donating blood to the mosquitoes. He still had to work on the walls and roof, but just being finished with the frame made Binson feel as if he had built a palace.

The cool sea breeze blew through the trees. Binson covered the ground with dry grass to prevent dampness and to keep warm. He lay on the soft grass bed and stretched himself, muttering.

"What's a fancy villa good for anyway. One should know the value of living the simple life. I will be content with poverty and delight in the Way, sing of the wind and moon, and live with integrity……."

It turned out one house was not enough. In order to prepare for the rainy season he had to have a storehouse to stock wood and food in. The interior of the triangular cabin was not big enough to store goods in.

"I wish there was a real estate agent. Then I would rent a flat even if I

---

donate (동) 기증하다
breeze (명) 산들바람
delight (명) 즐거움
integrity (명) 정직, 성실
goods (명) 상품, 물건
flat (명) 아파트
cut off 차단하다
That way the rain would fall down the sides without

leaking into the cabin 부사구 that way가 조건절로 쓰인 것으로 해석한다
at this rate 이런 식으로. 이 부사절도 조건절로 해석할 것
stretch oneself 기지개를 켜다
turn out (that) ~으로 판명나다, 결과가 ~이 되다
The interior of the triangular cabin was not big enough to store goods in → 전치사 in은 주어와 연결된다

had to walk around a lot to find it⋯⋯."

From the next day Binson decided to divide work by day and night. During the day he would gather food, and work on the house at night. It wasn't wise to do hard labor under the strong sun.

Binson the Hercules

"You rascals! Wait till I get my hands on any of you⋯⋯."

It was already high noon since he had started this hide-and-seek with the fish. He had been full of hope that he would have fish for his next meal when he started out toward the brook. But the fish were too quick for Binson's clumsy hands. There were a couple of times he grabbed one, but then it just slipped away.

At last Binson gave up on catching fish with his bare hands and sat on a rock by the side of the brook. His feet were wrinkled from standing in the water all morning.

'My feet have been soaked so good I could easily scrub off dirt.'

Binson rubbed his ankle with his finger then put his feet back in the water, shaking his head. There was a strip of filth on the tip of his finger. It reminded him of buckwheat noodles, which made him even hungrier.

He felt something move above his feet. As he looked inside the water, he could see a small fish swimming below the rock he was sitting on.

Binson crouched to look under the rock. He could see three or four

---

rascal (명) 강도, 악당
high noon 정오
brook (명) 시내(= creek)
wrinkle (동) 주름을 잡다
soak (동) 젖다, 담그다
filth (명) 때, 쓰레기

buckwheat noodle 메밀국수
crouch (동) 쭈그려 앉다
to do hard labor = to do laborhard = to work hard
scrub off 문질러 없애다
Binson crouched to look under the rock 쭈그려 앉아
  바위 밑을 살피다(내려 해석하는 것이 좋다)

fish moving back and forth between the rocks. It seemed to be the fishes' playground. Maybe it was just him, but it seemed like the fins swaying in the water were mocking him.

'Try and catch me. If you do I'll give you delicious fish pie······'

Annoyed, Binson threw a small pebble into the water. But even if Chanho Park were to throw the pebble, it could not maintain speed inside the water. The pebble slowly sank to the bottom. Even more frustrated, Binson stood up and looked around him for a big piece of rock.

"I will wreck your playground to pieces."

Binson picked up the rock and threw it at the entrance where the fish were going in and out. Thump-. With a thick thud water splashed around the rock. Feeling a throb in his hands, Binson muttered woefully.

"What am I doing boasting my strength to some fish······."

That moment, Binson's eyes widened as big as a baseball. Fish were floating in the water still wobbling from the shock. He first thought that the fish were protesting against this tyranny, but he soon realized what was happening. The fish had been knocked unconscious from the blow!

'Haha, what luck!'

Binson quickly picked up the fish and put them in the plastic bag. If they were to wake up all the fish would go into alert and hide. After filling up the plastic bag, he murmured softly, feeling a bit guilty.

"You shouldn't have teased me like that. It's not smart to tease someone bigger than you·······."

Fish lost in the maze

Binson roasted the fish and had the first nutritious meal since he got stranded. The fish came to their senses and realized that things had changed, but it was too late for them. No matter how hard they flapped their fins they were already too far away from their home playground.

The salted fish was different from clam even from the smell. Binson gorged himself with the fish, even chewing on the bone. He had grown tired of the clam he had eaten for days. Burp—. Binson picked his teeth

fin (명) 지느러미
pebble (명) 조약돌
frustrated (형) 실망한, 약이 오른
wreck (동) 파괴하다
thud (명) 쿵 → With a thick thud 쿵소리를 내면서
throb (명) 떨림, 진동(= vibration)
woefully (부) 비통하게, 슬픈 마음으로
wobble (동) 흔들거리다
tease (동) 놀리다
nutritious meal 영양식

had been knocked unconscious 충격을 받아 무의식 상태가 되다 → 기절하다
You shouldnt have teased me like that 나를 그렇게 놀리지 말았어야지!
came to their senses 의식을 차리다, 정신을 차리다
No matter how hard ~아무리 열심히 ~해도(양보절 = Though~)
gorge himself with 게걸스레 먹다
tired of 싫증나다 cf) tired with ~로 지치다

with the bones of the fish he had just eaten. How cruel.

"Today I was lucky. They don't always play under the rock······."

Binson was cruel sometimes, but he could also be modest. He knew that it was pure luck that the fish had been knocked unconscious. Creating an earthquake in the water could not be a secure means of obtaining food. He had to find a more reliable and effective way to catch fish.

"I will use the troop disposition technique of the old Chinese novels. I will make a maze and trap the fish inside. They're not smart enough to escape."

<Fishing maze>

Binson went immediately to work, to help with digestion. He already had enough material to build a maze. He was going to tie the branches he had gathered to make a storehouse. They would become the walls of the fishing maze instead. After moving the piles of branches, he thought what shape the maze should be.

"Should it be the shape of a heart? Or a 'V'? Or maybe a star?"

At last an elaborate maze was complete at the banks of the brook. While he was working another idea had struck him. He would make the same maze in the sea too.

"Some fish swim to shallow waters with the tide. I will make a fish pound at low tide as far in as possible, and by the time of the next low tide, it will be full of fish. Hehe I can't help it. I'm a genius."

Now that it was stimulated, Binson's brain began to work faster.

'Many fish may not enter with a maze alone. I have to put something to lure them in. The best way to lure animals is food······. So, what do

---

modest (형) 겸손한, 얌전한
secure (형) 안전한. a secure means of obtaining food 식량을 확보하는 확실한 방법
maze (명) 미로→ the fishing maze 물고기용 미로 → 어살
lure (동) 유혹하다, 유인하다
the troop disposition technique 병력배치법, 진법(陣法)

a fish pound 물고기 잡는 어망
as far in as possible 가능한한 안쪽으로 멀리
by the time of ~할 때쯤
I have to put something to lure them in = I have to put something (which) will lure them in = I have to put something in which will lure them

fish feed on?"

Binson went out to the tidal flat and caught some lugworm. He also decided to use the fish eyes and entrails he had thrown away by the fire. He used the bones of the fish to use as the needle to hold the bait. Binson was trying to catch fish by luring them with their friends' remains. How mean.

The next day. Binson gleefully scooped out the fish wandering about in the maze. There were only small fish in the fish pound in the sea, but in the brook, there were some big fish too. Stroking the sleek back of the fish Binson murmured in a dreamy voice.

"It would have been great if there was a mermaid caught in the maze······."

Binson goes gathering herbs

After the fish, Binson now went on a hunt for fresh vegetables.

Of course sashimi was much more expensive than vegetables, but you can't live only on fish unless you're a polar bear. Vegetables are necessary not only for taste but to maintain a balanced diet.

There were countless plants in the forest but not all of them were edible. He could have food poisoning, or even worse he could get poisoned. Binson decided that he would try only those vegetables that he knew or that looked similar to those he had seen his mother buy.

"This is bracken so I can eat it······. Yes, this is mugwort. Uhm, This looks like Korean lettuce. Let's try some."

Binson wandered about in the woods and collected various wild vegetables. Among them were vegetables he had often seen such as bracken and mugwort, and some he didn't know the names of but somehow looked familiar. Unfortunately he could not find his favorite, the roots of a bellflower.

"Now I know that song 'White bellflower deep deep in the mountain' does not count on this island."

Binson decided he would try one kind of vegetable each day.

If he tried several at the same time and became sick, he wouldn't know what had caused it. When trying the vegetables, he sliced them to small pieces and ate only a little. If it tasted or smelled funny, he spit it out and rinsed his mouth.

After a few days he had picked out several vegetables he could safely eat. He also knew what part tasted better among the leaves, the stem, or the root. Not only that, he knew which to boil for a while and which to parboil. Now Binson's diet had improved from just clam to a more balanced meal of fish and vegetables.

<Edible plants. From left to right, easter lily, sow thistle,
Lactuca indica var. laciniata>

All life forms absorb nutrition from outside source to create energy and sustain life. The human body needs carbohydrates, proteins, and fat. Add vitamins and minerals to the 'three basic nutrients' and you have the 'five basic nutrients.' A diet of 55% carbohydrates, 15% proteins and 35% fats is ideal.

Carbohydrate is the main source of energy and an important fuel that moves the central nervous system. In particular, glucose that is produced by breaking down carbohydrate is necessary in maintaining the nerve system functional.

Protein is the basic component of a cell and is a must-have substance to sustain life. The word 'protein' originates from the Greek word 'proteios' which means 'of first importance.' Proteins are the main substance of muscles, organs, the skin, hair and nails. It composes about 16% of the human body, second only to water.

Fats are a concentrated source of energy, which gives 9Kcal per gram. This is more than twice of carbohydrates and proteins. All excess nutrients are stored in the form of fat. On the other hand, when energy consumption is greater than intake, fat is decomposed to generate energy.

Vitamins do not generate energy but they enable the three nutrients to work properly. Only about 20mg is needed daily, but as vitamins cannot be synthesized within the body, it must be taken from outside sources. Minerals are not a source of energy either, but it is necessary to control body functions. Calcium and phosphorus are the main components of bones and teeth.

If any of the five basic nutrients are insufficient, it will cause all sorts of illnesses.

Below are the basic food groups necessary for a balanced diet.

- Group 1(proteins): meat, fish, eggs, beans, cheese, tofu
- Group 2(calcium): milk, dairy products, anchovy, ice cream, shrimp, yogurt
- Group 3(vitamins and minerals): vegetables, fruits, tomato ketchup
- Group 4(carbohydrates): grains, potato, bread, biscuits, chocolates
- Group 5(fats): milk fat, various animal fats, walnuts, butter, margarine, sesame

Toadstool or not, that is the question

"Wow, this place is full of mushrooms."

Binson's eyes widened. He had found a nook of the forest covered with all sorts of mushrooms, displayed as if in a mushroom store. Dark brown mushroom, reddish mushroom, whitish mushroom, spotted mushroom……. The size varied too, from those the size of his fingernails to those as big as his fist. If the place under the rock had been fish's playground, this must be fungi's playground.

Binson had not eaten mushrooms since he learned in elementary school that mushrooms were a form of fungus. But he knew that mushrooms were highly nutritious. Mother had often scolded him for not

---

funny (형) 의심스러운, 메스꺼운
spit out 내뱉다
rinse (동) 헹구다, 씻어내다
parboil (동) 데치다, 잠깐 동안 삶다
A balanced diet 균형식
carbohydrate (명) 탄수화물
mineral (명) 무기질
basic nutrient 기본 영양소
glucose 포도당
must-have (형) 필수의 → a must-have substance 필수성분
intake (명) 섭취량
decompose (동) 분해시키다
synthesize (동) 합성하다

phosphorus (명) 인
dairy products 유제품
anchovy (명) 멸치
Toadstool (명) 독버섯
nook (명) 구석
fungus (명) 버섯 → 복수는 fungi
knew which to boil for a while and which to parboil
  에서 know = tell
the main source of energy 에너지원
He had found a nook of the forest covered with all sorts of mushrooms, 시제(과거완료)의 사용으로 보아 앞 문장의 이유를 설명한다
Mother had often scolded him for not eating them
  scold A for B : B를 이유로 A를 꾸짖다

eating them.

"Do you know how expensive matsutake mushroom is? Why did you bring your lunch back? Did you beg from your friends for side dishes again?"

After being lost in thought for a while, Binson finally decided that he would follow his mother's bidding and eat the mushroom. But he could not just eat any mushroom. Some mushrooms are highly poisonous and could be fatal. He had survived too long to die to a fungus.

"There must be poisonous mushrooms here······ what should I do?"

Binson thought of the comic book heroes he had read of when he was in middle school. The guy and the girl were lost in the woods and ate only dull-colored mushrooms, saying those with fancy colors were mostly poisonous. They survived that way for two months until they were rescued. The title was something like ⟨Romance in the mushroom field⟩.

"Can I trust the comic book? All the mushrooms mother had cooked were also dull in color······ The writer of the comic book wouldn't have just made it up. Alright, let's trust what he said."

Like the comic mania he was, he decided to believe the comic book. He took samples of the mushrooms. He would try small amounts everyday, just like he did with the vegetables. Even if it were poisonous, he didn't think one small piece would kill him.

Some mushrooms were dark pink in the gills.

'Oops, better be careful. From the fancy color, it must be poisonous. You can't fool me.'

Binson didn't even go close to the pink mushroom lest he be poisoned from touching it.

Some mushrooms had what looked like boils at the roots. Binson excluded these too. He had suddenly remembered what his father had told him.

"Remember, foundation is very important. A family with weak roots cannot produce talent. Our No family is a noble family with deep roots and has produced many great scholars for generations······ and so on and so forth······ In short, Binson you are a mutant in our family line."

Binson brought some samples of the mushrooms except those that looked suspicious. He then put some water in the tin and made a fire.

Then he tore the samples into thin strips.

---

bidding (명) 명령, 가르침
gill (명) 버섯 뒷면의 주름, 아가미
boil (명) 부스럼, 종기
mutant 돌연 변이
being lost in thought (= lose onseself in thought)

깊은 생각에 잠겨버리다
read of ~을 읽고 알다
made it up = make up the comic book. make up
구성하다

Inside the stipe some had nasty looking black spots.

'Reminds me of AIDS.'

Binson quickly threw it away. It reminded him of the film he had seen about AIDS.

After screening everything that looked suspicious, he was left with five or six kinds. Binson thought that the finalists all looked somewhat familiar. They looked very similar to those he had seen inside mother's shopping bag. Round shaped matsutake, flat oyster mushroom, shiitake mushroom which was dark outside and white inside, thin and long

enoki······ It turns out that edible mushrooms are all alike anywhere in the world.

"I should have just picked only those that I knew from the start······ By the way, why isn't there some turkey tails that's supposed to be so good for you?"

Throwing the shredded boiled mushrooms into his mouth, he suddenly remembered his days in high school.

'I had cut the sides and back of my hair just before the hair inspection, and Malsuk had laughed at me all day.'

"Hey you look just like a mushroom. With your hair like that, it's just hilarious!"

He suddenly missed Malsuk and her snag tooth.

stipe (명) 줄기, 자루
nasty (형) 흉칙스런, 불결한
finalist (명) 마지막까지 남은 것(사람) → 결승전 진출자
oyster mushroom 느타리버섯
shiitake (mushroom) 표고버섯(이것도 일본어)
shred (동) 잘게 찢다

hilarious (형) 유쾌한, 즐거운
snag tooth 덧니
similar to ~와 비슷한, 유사한
you look just like a mushroom 꼭 버섯처럼 보인다 *
　형용사일 때는 you look pale 창백해 보인다

setting a trap

Rustle—. It sounds like something is moving in the woods. Startled, Binson hid behind a big tree and held his breath. He stared in the direction the noise had come from. His hands holding a club was wet with sweat.

"What was that? It definitely wasn't the sound of breeze. A tiger? A snake? A rat? Or······ could it be a cannibal?"

Countless thoughts flew threw his mind.

'If it's a predatory animal I can't beat it with just this club unless it's sick or weak. Can I believe the Aesop's Fable where the fellow survived by pretending to be dead? If I run like mad a snake won't probably get me. But if it's a cannibal······ ugh.'

His hair stood on end as his blood curled. He had just envisioned himself being thrown into a huge boiling pot.

'I mustn't think of such things······.'

Binson closed his eyes firmly and thought of a comic he had read when in high school. The hero had been caught by cannibals then fell in love with a girl of the tribe and escaped with her help. The title was something like ⟨Cannibal's First Love⟩.

That moment, something passed by in front of Binson. His knees went weak when he realized what had made the noise.

'Stupid Binson. You mean to tell me you were scared because of that?'

What came out of the woods was a brown hare with a thick coat.

"I must catch it. I really must catch it······."

Binson thought hard on how he could catch the hare.

'Should I ask for a duel and catch it alive?'

Unfortunately a rabbit cannot understand human language. Even if it did, Binson didn't speak island tongue, and the hare probably wouldn't understand English. Even if the rabbit did understand, if it declined the challenge, it would be no use.

"I could set a trap there and wait. Animals usually take the same route, so I will be able to catch it some time."

But the problem was how to set the trap. There were no stores where

---

Rustle (명) 바스락대는 소리
cannibal (명) 식인종
pretend (동) ~인 척하다. by pretending to be dead 죽은 척함으로써
tribe (명) 부족, 종족
scared (형) 겁먹은, 두려워하는
alive (형) 살아 있는 catch it alive(산채로 잡다)에서 alive
hold his breath 숨을 죽이다. 숨을 멈추다
a predatory animal 맹수 = predator

His hair stood on end 머리카락이 곤두서다
his blood curled 피가 요동치다 → 소름이 돋다
He had just envisioned himself being thrown into a huge boiling pot 그 자신이 팔팔 끓는 가마솥에 내던져지는 장면을 떠올렸다 (동명사가 쓰인 것에 유의할 것)
His knees went weak 무릎에 힘이 빠지다 (= he has got weak knees) 는 부사로 해석되지만 품사는 형용사이다
set the trap 덫을 설치하다

he could buy one, or any forge where he could make some pieces of metal. He tried hard to remember the structure of the mousetrap his father had brought home one day, but all he could remember was the sad looking eyes of the rat that was caught in it.

'I became the black sheep of the family for a while when I tried to persuade everyone to let the rat go free.'

"Whimper. Let poor Mickey Mouse go."

"Binson come to your senses. That's not Mickey Mouse, that's a rat."

Binson opened his eyes again after thinking of the dear faces he missed so much. From the light in his eyes, it seemed like he had an idea on how to catch the hare.

Binson had thought of two things. One was a snare, the other a pit. He

flexible twig that will not break

<Snare for hunting>

remembered the snare thanks to a TV documentary on illegal poachers, and he remembered the pit when he thought of the pit he had dug with his friends to play pranks on adults in the neighborhood. He would dig a pit in the trail on the hill near the neighborhood where people came out to take a walk, and cover it with grass - then adults would fall into them as they passed by.

Binson twisted some tough grass and made a long cord. He made a round snare, and tied the other end to a branch, letting the snare touch the ground. The diameter of the snare was just enough for a hare to pass by. He made a lose knot so that when a hare was caught by the body or leg, the snare would tighten.

But when he actually tied the snare to a branch, the cord hung loose and the round snare became narrow and longish in shape. A hare wouldn't be able to pass through that unless it had starved for a long time. After thinking for a while, Binson finally came up with the idea of propping two sticks on the ground and opening the mouth of the snare by

---

forge (명) 대장간
pit (명) 함정
illegal poachers 밀렵꾼들
prank (명) 장난 play pranks on ~에게 장난치다, ~을 놀리다
longish (형) 길쭉한
starve (동) 굶다

the black sheep of the family 가족의 검은 양 → 외톨이
it seemed like + 절 ~과 같이 생각되다(=It seemed that ~)
the idea of propping two sticks on the ground and opening the mouth of the snare : 동격의 of로 두 동명사절(propping ~와 opening~)은 idea와 동격이다

placing it lightly on each stick.

After completing the snare, he put his feet in it to test if it worked. The knot was pulled and tightened on his ankles.

"This will do."

Binson untied the knot with a satisfied look on his face. Now if a wild rabbit even as much as touched the snare, it would become handcuffs······ or fetters to be more accurate. Only humans have hands, after all.

He decided to dig a pit a bit away from the snare. He had in mind the fact that animals follow the same trail most of the time. If the hare took a walk through the same trail everyday like Binson thought, it would have to pass two obstacles to get home safely.

At first he was going to dig a pit big enough to hold one or two rabbits. But he changed his mind as he started out on his plan. He may as well make it big enough for other animals to fall in. Deer, boar, or at least an old donkey would be nice.

"If I catch a deer I will brew its antlers, if I catch a boar I will have a barbecue, and if it's a donkey I will tame it and ride it. Just like Don Quixote."

Binson dug a pit big enough to hold an elephant and lay some thin twigs on it, and covered it with leaves and grass. Then he brought some dirt and threw it on top. It was to camouflage the trap.

He thought of placing pointed bamboo spikes before covering the trap, but then changed his mind, thinking it was too cruel.

'This is an uninhabited island, not the killing fields.'

Everything was ready.

'I will have to come everyday to check on the snare and pit beginning from tomorrow.'

Binson's mouth watered at the thought of sizzling meat, then he muttered.

"What if a rabbit and lion were to fall in the pit together? The lion would eat up the rabbit."

---

handcuff (명) 수갑
fetter (명) 족쇄
brew (동) 끓이다, 주조하다
antler (명) 뿔. its antlers → 녹용
tame (동) 길들이다
dirt (명) 흙
if it worked는 test의 목적어로 명사절이다.
most of the time 거의 언제나

may as well V ~해도 좋다, ~하는 편이 낫다
an old donkey would be nice 늙은 당나귀라도 괜찮아
It was to camouflage the trap 함정을 위장하려는 것이었다(be to V)
changed his mind 생각을 바꾸다
Binson's mouth watered at the thought 그 생각에 빈손의 입에 침이 고이다
What if ~하면 어떻게 될까?

\<Trap for hunting\>

Binson's treasure chest, the tidal flat

The wide tidal flat was a precious treasure chest for Binson. Numerous animals lived there following the laws of nature. Every day at low tide Binson came out and gathered fresh sea food in the bag he had made with twisted grass.

Clam was most abundant. There seemed to be scores of different kinds of clam some the size of his fists and some the size of the nails of his little finger. There were littleneck clam, mussel, ark shell, venus clam, tusk shell······ Some of them were big enough to be a few hundred years old.

Another delight Binson found was the crabs. There were big and small crabs walking sideways here and there. Some hid in the ground with only their eyes protruding like periscopes. When Binson came near, they would quickly hide their eyes. Further inside the flat, he would sometimes catch crab the size of Tyson's fists.

At low tide, seaweeds such as wakame and tangleweed were everywhere. Binson gathered wakame, washed it and let it dry in the sun.

Crisp dry seaweed is very nutritious and good as a snack too.

"Hey, it's a long-legged octopus!"

Sea birds strolling nearby fluttered and flew away, startled at Binson's

treasure chest 보물상자
score (명) 20, **scores of** ~수십 가지의
littleneck clam 대합
Crisp (형) 파삭파삭한
flutter (동) 퍼덕거리다
following the laws of nature 자연의 법칙을 따라서

with only their eyes protruding like periscopes 잠망경처럼 돌출된 눈만으로(양태의 부사이다. 전치사 with와 동명사구에서 판단이 가능하다)
Sea birds strolling nearby = Sea birds (which are) strolling nearby. 결국 분사절의 형용사적 용법이다

outburst. Binson looked down at his prize at his feet in amazement. He had happened on a bald long-legged octopus while trying to find some blue crab.

"That's odd. I thought these lived in the water."

That's not true. Some long-legged octopus live in the water, but some live buried in the tidal flat, like the one Binson had found. The most famous in Korea is the thin legged kind of Mokpo harbor. The home of this type of long-legged octopus is not the South Sea, but the tidal flat of the Youngsan River flat. But Binson who had lived only in Seoul all his life couldn't have known this.

While trying to find the rest of the long-legged octopus' friends, Binson found a large turban shell.

'Wow, an octopus and now a turban shell? Today I will have the best seafood soup.'

Binson's mouth watered with the thought. The turban shell that was enjoying its mud sauna felt oncoming danger and coiled inside its shell, but it was in vain.

'Hehe, you poor thing. Hide as much as you like, it's still only in your shell.'

Picking up the shell, he suddenly remembered the time he had gone on a blind date when he first entered the university. The long haired girl's name was "Sora." When he had first met her she had smiled sweetly at him, making him feel giddy inside. But when they went to a night club later that night she had left with a cold look on her face. Why did she leave like that? Binson answered his own question with regret.

"I shouldn't have had that seasoned hairy triton······."

The tidal flat, neither land nor sea but a third zone

A tidal flat is the vast, flat shore of an estuary where the sea water flows in and out. The mud and sand that flows from the river sinks in the shore that meets the estuary of the river. When the deposit of mud and sand accumulates for a long time, a tidal flat—which is neither land nor sea—is created.

In order for a tidal flat to be formed, the waves must be mild, the land must be flat, the sea should be shallow, and there should be considerable gap between high and low tide. There are only a few places in the world where all these conditions are met, such as the western shoreline of Korea, the shoreline of the North Sea in Europe, the shores of Georgia in east USA, and the estuary of the Amazon in South America.

The tidal flat can be composed of sand, mud, or a mixture of the two. In order for the mud or sand to accumulate, the flow of the sea water should be much gentler than the flat, because the mud is lighter and finer than sand.

There are numerous creatures living in the tidal flat. The most common are lugworms, crabs and shellfish, which together comprise about 90% of the living organisms of a tidal flat. A tidal flat composed of mud contains a lot of organic material, and is inhabited mostly by lugworms and crabs. A flat composed of sand is the home of many shellfish. The total area of Korea's tidal flat is about 2,800㎢, which is about 3% of the total area of tidal flat in the world. However with recent reclamation and change of land use, more than 60% has been damaged.

Tools for a cultured life

After moving to the new home, Binson's living settled down considerably. He had enough fish, vegetables and seafood as nourishment, and he could sleep well at night since he had built his cabin. Since he had regained some peace of mind he started to make various living utensils whenever he had a spare moment.

What he needed most was kitchenware. When he had lived only on clam and fish it was enough to cook them on the fire, but as the amount and variety of foods increased, he definitely needed something to cook them in. Also in order to store food he had to make several baskets and pots.

Binson shaped the mud from the tidal flat to make kitchenware. But

---

harbor (명) 항구
oncoming (형) 다가오는, 접근하는
estuary (명) 강의 어귀, 하구
However (부) 그러나
reclamation 개발, 간척사업
utensil (명) 용구, 기구 living utensils → 생활도구
the one Binson had found에서 the one = the octopus
felt oncoming danger 위험이 다가오는 것을 느끼다
which is neither land nor sea 육지도 아니고 바다도 아
닌

In order for a tidal flat to be formed 갯벌이 형성되기
위해서
gap between high and low tide 간만의 차이
such as 예를들면
be composed of ~으로 구성되다
A tidal flat composed of mud 진흙으로 된 갯벌
settle down 안정되다
whenever he had a spare moment 여유 있는 시간이
생길 때마다, 틈틈이

the earthenware Binson dried in the sun would crack when he put it on top of the fire. Thus he could use them only to store vegetables or dried fish, but he could not cook anything in them.

joints

thick bamboo

cut

bamboo fork

bowl

cut outside the joints and
you have a plate or pot

water

fire

"If I bake the earthenware, wouldn't it harden a little?"

But there was no kiln or stove on this island. He tried digging a hole in the ground and making a fire inside, but the wares broke before they were baked properly.

Earthenware cannot be made just by baking. The clay has to be very fine of less than 0.01mm in diameter. The wares must be dried in the shade then baked gradually raising the temperature. Then it has to be glazed and dried, then baked again. When there is no glaze available you can use the ashes from pine needles or straw dissolved in water.

But Binson who had only played with clay a couple of times at elementary school didn't know these facts.

Binson finally gave up firing earthenware and thought of another way. The new material he discovered was bamboo. He cut the bamboo at the joints then split it open vertically. As bamboo is hollow inside, it made a nice vessel. Bamboo didn't burn so easily and it was perfect for boiling clam soup or cooking vegetables. Fortunately there was plenty of bamboo in the forest as thick as his arm.

---

earthenware (명) 토기
crack (동) 균열되다, 갈라지다
harden (동) 단단해지다 ← hard + en(동사형 어미)

kiln (명) 가마
a couple of times 두어 번

After solving his need for kitchenware, he now went on to make some stoneware. He was going to make a stone axe and knife to use when chopping wood and hunting. The pocketknife was all but useless for these purposes. After all he wasn't going to need it as a symbol of chastity like the women of the Chosun dynasty did.

First he needed a hard rock as material. He remembered trying to make a fire by using a flint stone and looked around the brook carefully. Fortunately there were some quartz of appropriate size among the pebbles and rocks.

First he picked a flat rock to make into a knife and a longish one to make an axe. Then he struck down hard with a small piece of rock. Every time the rocks hit each other, sparks and small bits of broken rocks flew about.

'This feels like welding with rocks.'

Wiping the sweat on his forehead, Binson muttered somewhat regrettably.

"If I had found these earlier, I wouldn't have had such a hard time making a fire."

Binson entered the forest with the stone axe and headed straight to a pine tree he had picked out earlier. The reason he wanted the pine tree was because of its resin at the stump and roots. Resinous pine knots were used as lamp fuel from old times.

Binson swung his axe vigorously, to test its power. The pine tree that must have lived a proud lonely life for hundreds of years on this island had no choice but to give up part of its body to a young novice.

Putting the knot in his bag, Binson muttered in excitement.

"From tonight I will have moody lighting in the house."

When Binson returned to the cabin he drove a piece of wood into the ground and tied a small saucer on it. Then he placed the chopped pine resin on the dish and lit it. The gloomy cabin lit up, and soon the fragrance filled the air. There was too much smoke because the resin had not been dried enough, but that didn't matter. Just the fact that he had lighting made him feel warm at the heart.

---

chastity (명) 정절
quartz (명) 석영. quartz of appropriate size 적당한 크기
　의 석영
resin (명) 송진, 수지
stump (명) 그루터기, 밑동
vigorously (부) 기운차게
novice (명) 신출내기, 풋내기
saucer (명) 접시
fragrance (명) 향기
lighting (명) 조명 → 등불
went on to make some stoneware go on to V 이어서
　다음에 ~하다, cf) go on + ~ing 계속해서 하다
all but = only

a flint stone 부싯돌
Every time the rocks hit each other = whenever the
　rocks ~
feels like welding ~하는 기분이다, ~하는 것을 느끼다
The pine tree that must have lived a proud lonely
life for hundreds of years on this island 이 섬에서 수
　백 년 동안 고고하게 살았던 소나무. must 다음에 완료형
　(have + 과거 분사)이 올 경우에는 보통 '~에 틀림없다'
　의 뜻
had no choice but to V ~할 수밖에 없다 (but= except)
the fact that he had lighting　the fact = he had
　lighting

It was dawn. Binson could not sleep all night, and he finally sat up. His shadow was flickering to the dancing lamp light.

'When I was young I used to make pictures with the shadows of my hands against the candle light·······.'

With this memory, he crossed his thumbs together and opened his

palm and made a figure of a bird on the wall. A small bird flew up on the earthen wall of the cabin on this lonely island. As Binson moved his hand the bird flapped its wings.

'I wish I had wings like that bird. Then I would fly home······.'

That day he dreamt of becoming a bird and flying in the sky. Then he screamed and wailed his arms and legs. A ferocious eagle that looked just like Malsuk came after him.

Binson gets meat and pelt

"God! Didn't you hear my prayer? I prayed so hard for just one rabbit······"

Why did God give him two when he had only asked for one? When he came out early morning, a gray rabbit was caught at the ankles in the snare, and another was lying flat on the ground of the pit.

---

wail (동) 울부짖다, 비명을 지르다
came after 뒤쫓아 오다
another = another (rabbit)

Then = if I had wings like that bird
a gray rabbit was caught at the ankles in the snare
잿빛 토끼가 덫에 발목이 묶이다

'Hehe, two in one night……'

Binson's mouth opened wide. He felt like he had won a lottery.

"Well, what am I going to do with them?"

Binson was troubled. These were not pets but food.

In other words, he had to kill them.

'But how could I when they are looking at me that way?'

Binson shut his eyes and shook his head. He had only thought of catching and eating the rabbit but not killing them. Now he was at a loss.

But Binson soon realized that he was not in a situation to free animals that were caught in the traps. After all, the clam and fish he had eaten until now were also precious life forms. However piteous they may be, their lives could not be worth more than his.

"Ok. I gotta do what I gotta do."

Having made up his mind Binson breathed deeply and raised the club high in the air.

Binson hung the hind legs of the rabbit to a tree branch. Then he split open the skin at the hind leg, pushed in the knife between the meat and pelt, and slowly skinned the rabbit. The pelt came off more easily than expected.

Next it was time to separate the head from the body. For a moment he felt a pang of guilt even more than when he had clubbed the rabbit, but he shut his eyes and picked up the knife again.

After the first rich meal he had had in a long while, Binson closely examined the rabbit pelt. To use the leather he had to tan it first but there was no chemical on this island.

"How can I make this into a fur coat? I have no choice. I will first try soaking it in salt water."

Binson removed the inside of the pelt of all meat and fat, and immersed it in seawater. If it didn't soften the pelt, at least it would prevent rotting. Then he soaked it in flowing water to rinse off the salt. But the leather was still stiff.

"Argh, who cares. If I can't make a jacket with it, I'll just use it as bed sheet."

Binson gave up on making a jacket and laid the pelt on the floor.

---

split (동) 찢다 split open 찢어서 벌리다
skin (동) 가죽을 벗기다
pelt (명) 가죽(= skin)
tan (동) 무두질하다
felt like he had won a lottery 복권에 당첨된 기분이었다
feel like + 절 ~한 느낌이다
was at a loss 어찌할 바를 모르다 (= puzzled)
However piteous they may be = though they may

be so piteous
it was time to V ~할 시간이다
a pang of guilt 죄책감
removed the inside of the pelt of all meat and fat
가죽 안쪽에서 살과 지방을 제거하다 : remove A of B A
에서 B를 제거하다
prevent rotting 부패하는 것을 방지하다 (prevent + ~ing)

'No one's here to look at me anyway.'

Then it suddenly reminded him of another of Aesop's fables. After failing to obtain the grapes, "What's good to eat sour grapes anyway," the foolish fox had complained. But Binson shook his head and muttered in a firm voice.

"I'm not a fox. Malsuk always said I was a wolf."

But was there really no way to make a leather jacket on this island? Not true. If you soak the skin of an oak tree you can get a tanning solution. The more concentrated and higher the temperature of the solution, the more effective it will be. After soaking the pelt in the solution for about ten days, rinse it and let it dry in the shade with the inside of the pelt facing up, and you get a nice pelt coat.

Lying down on the fur sheet felt much cozier than lying on the grass bed. Binson decided he would collect the pelts whenever he caught some animals and take them with him when he escaped from the island.

'I will make not only a coat but also a wallet and belt. It will be total fashion.'

Then he remembered the argument he had had with his mother last winter.

"Mom, buy me a fur coat"

"Be quiet. I have no money."

"Then buy me a leather jacket."

"Quiet, I said! You look good without it. I mean it."

Making smoked meat

As food grew abundant Binson needed a better way to store food. In the damp and hot weather, meat and fish would get spoiled before he ate them all.

"I will make jerked meat and dried fish. They won't spoil as easily when they're dry."

When Binson caught rabbits from time to time he boiled the meat and salted it in the seawater then let it dry in the sun. As for the fish he took out the intestines and gills that spoils more easily, salted the meat then hung them on branches to dry. After a few days Binson's cabin was

---

effective (형) 효과적인
pelt coat 모피코트
jerk (동) 육포로 만들다
spoil (동) 상하다
intestines (명) 내장, 복수형태로 쓰이지만 단수 취급
gill (명) 아가미

a tanning solution 무두질용 용액
with the inside of the pelt facing up 가죽의 안쪽을 겉으로 향하게 해서
and you get a nice pelt coat 그럼 당신은 멋진 모피를 가지게 된다. 명령문, and~ 구문이다
As for~ ~에 관해서는

surrounded by hanging fish, just like in a fishing village.

But Binson was not very satisfied with this method. Dried fish tasted ok, but jerked meat didn't taste as good as roasted meat. Binson used to get the eye from his friends in restaurants because he would only eat side dishes that tasted good. For Binson eating something that didn't taste good was as bad as starving.

"Smoke! That's it."

Binson, who had been staring at the smoke from the bonfire, blurted out excitedly.

His eyes sparkled again in a long time.

"I will make smoked meat. Tender, fragrant smoked meat."

It was a great idea. Smoked meat tastes much better than jerked beef, and can be stored for a long time without spoiling. Antiseptic substances seep into the meat from the smoke. He remembered the smoked pork side dish of the pub he used to frequent, and immediately went to work.

First he dug a hole about 1 meter deep. He made a fire at the bottom then lay twigs in the form of a grill about 70cm from the ground. He put sliced meat on top of the grill then covered the top of the hole with leaves and grass so that smoke would not leak. Now all he had to do was wait till the meat was fully smoked······.

"Uh oh, I made a mistake again."

Binson opened the lid of the hole, clicking his tongue. He should have burned wet wood to get a lot of smoke but he had put dry firewood. He had failed in sending a rescue signal when the ship had appeared last time, and he had made the same mistake twice.

Binson took out the grill that he had made.

Then he put freshly chopped wood on top of the fire. Thick smoke billowed from the hole with a sizzling sound. Covering the hole again, Binson muttered as if to scold himself.

"I should learn to do things right the first time. It's not smart wasting precious energy this way."

Having made a pot full of smoked meat, Binson felt reassured. With this amount of food, he thought he would have enough through the rain.

---

blurt (동) 불쑥 말하다
Smoked meat 훈제고기
Antiseptic (형) 살균력을 지닌
seep (동) 스며들다, 침투하다
leak (동) 새어나오다
lid (명) 뚜껑
billow (동) 굽이치다
reassured (형) 안심하는, felt reassured 마음이 편안
　　해지다
a fishing village 어촌

For Binson eating something that didnt taste good was as bad as starving 빈손에게, 맛없는 것을 먹는 것은 굶는 것과 마찬가지로 괴로운 일이었다
stare at ~을 물끄러미 바라보다
a hole about 1 meter deep 약 1미터 깊이의 구멍
take out 드러내다, 꺼내다
with a sizzling sound 칙칙 소리를 내면서
as if to scold himself = as if he had scolded himself
It's smart wasting precious energy this way 동명사가 진주어, it는 가주어로 쓰인 구문이다

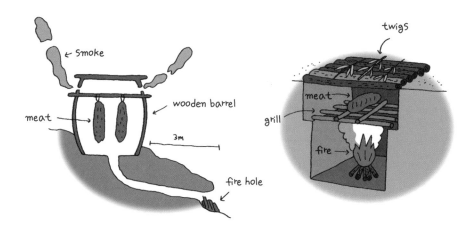

<Making smoked meat>

That night, Binson woke up startled to the sound of rain. It was pouring hard from the dark sky.

4

Blue days

The rain just wouldn't let up. The wind blew as if to blow away the whole cabin and the shore was raging with enormous waves. The noise of the rain, wind and the waves thundered in his ears like the special sound effects of a war movie.

Binson looked out woefully. It was dark as if it was dusk although it was only midday. The floor of the cabin was muddy from the rain that

---

muddy (형) 진창의
let up (비·눈 등이) 멎다, 약해지다
blow away (신산조각이 나도록) 때려 부수다

looked out 밖을 내다보다
from the rain that had leaked in 스며든 빗물 때문에

had leaked in.

He had lit a fire in the tin to keep the fire going but it was not enough to keep the damp from seeping in.

Plonk – . He heard a waterdrop fall. The rain that had leaked from the roof had fallen into the container. He had emptied the container just a while ago and now it was full of water again.

'I am already tired of being surrounded by sea water and now I have to put up with rain too?'

Binson slumped back down on the muddy floor, his face full of sorrow.

It rained in Binson's heart too. The dark sky made Binson glum.

'Will I ever get out of this place? I am struggling to survive but I could end up dying alone.'

The more questions he asked himself the more negative the answers became. A bud of doubt was growing in his mind, and the hard rain was its nourishment.

Perhaps it was because he had more time on his hands. Ever since the crash, Binson had been too busy trying to survive that he had no time to think of anything else.

But now that he had nothing to do because of the rain, weak thoughts began to nibble at his mind. The biggest threat to being stranded was not cold, thirst or hunger, but the boredom and stress that diminish the will to survive.

Binson sat vacantly all day, doing nothing. His face grew haggard by the day because he didn't eat properly. Island trapped in the sea, cabin trapped in the rain. Depression set in on the lonely island.

Despair comes with fear

Flash − . The dark sky lit up momentarily. Then a loud thunder shook the cabin. Binson had dozed off and now woke up startled. It was a deafening roar that made his spine chill.

"The lightning must have hit somewhere close."

---

slump (동) 쿵 떨어지다. slumped back down on ~에 털썩 주저앉다
glum (형) 침울한, 기분이 좋지 않은
nibble (동) 조금씩 갉아먹다
boredom (명) 권태, 지루함
vacantly (부) 하는 일 없이, 멍하게
haggard (형) 수척한, 초췌한 grew haggard by the day 나날이 수척해지다
deafening (형) 귀를 멍멍하게 하는

keep A form V ~ing A가 ~하는 것을 막다.
put up with 견디다(=endure)
his face full of sorrow 양태의 부사구로 with가 생략된 것이다
he had more time on his hands 시간적 여유를 갖다
doze off 선잠을 자다
that made his spine chill 등골을 오싹하게 만드는
the lightning must have hit somewhere close ← must have + pp의 용법

130

The lightning continued every few seconds. The sky flashed like the lighting in a nightclub and the earth shook as if there was an earthquake. The rainwater in the container spilled over from the tremor onto the cabin floor.

"Could the cabin get hit by lightning?"

Binson's spine chilled.

Lightning strikes the highest point. This hill is the highest point, and the cabin roof will be the first target. He had not made a lightning rod, and it was obvious what would happen if lightning were to strike the cabin.

The thunder drew closer. Binson tried to shake off his anxiety and counted the interval of the light and sound. 3 seconds, 2 seconds, 1 second······. As the lightning and thunder came at about the same time, his anxiety turned to fear.

'I have to get out, out of this cabin······.'

Binson ran out into the pouring rain.

---

tremor (명) 진동, 떨림 from the tremor 진동으로
every few seconds 몇 초 간격으로
The rainwater in the container spilled over from the tremor onto the cabin floor = from the tremor, the

rainwater in the container spilled over onto the cabin floor
a lightning rod 피뢰침
it was obvious +절 ~은 자명하다

But it was just as scary outside. The lightning was striking the earth like a giant tree root, thundering ceaselessly. He closed his eyes and covered his ears but he could still see and hear them. Every time the lightning struck, Binson's flinching shoulders became visible as if it was broad daylight.

'Do I really have to try to survive like this? Even if I did survive I will live alone on this island and die alone on this island. It might be better to just be hit by lightning and go quickly. Then at least I won't feel pain······.'

Binson crouched covering his head, and a deep sense of despair crept in.

The lightning let up after a long time. Binson wearily came back to the cabin, covered in muddy water. It was still raining hard.

The fire dies

"Come on, come back to life······ please!"

Binson tried hard to bring back the fire into life. The light in the tin had gone out while Binson had gone outside to escape from the lightning. Binson had diminished the fire before going to sleep, because too much smoke came from the damp firewood. And now the fire seemed gone.

If he lost the fire he wouldn't be able to make a fire again until the rain stopped and the sun came out. He had water and food but heating was the problem. It would be hard to get through the night without fire on the shore howling with wind and rain. Also, Binson had been out in the rain for a long time and his teeth were clattering with cold.

But Binson had another reason for being so anxious. To Binson the flick of the fire was the hope that he would escape soon. Since the first time he decided he would never let the fire die, two months had passed without once letting it go off. The fire had saved him from thirst and starvation. It had also been his distress signal he had set up in various places on the island. That precious fire was now fading.

---

scary (형) 무서운, 무시무시한
broad (형) 환한, 충만한. broad daylight 대낮
crouch (동) 몸을 웅크리다
clatter (동) 덜커덕 소리를 내다
It might be better to V ~하는 편이 더 나을지도 모른다
crouched covering his head 머리를 감싸고 몸을 웅크리다
creep in 스며들다
(being) covered in muddy water 흙탕물로 범벅인 된 채

The light in the tin had gone out 과거완료로 쓰인 것은 앞 사건의 이유를 설명
go out 꺼지다
get through the night 밤을 넘기다
reason for being so anxious. reason for~ ~에 대한 이유
the flick of the fire 불씨
go off 꺼지다 = go out

"I was wrong. I will cheer up. Please come back to life⋯⋯."

But it was in vain. The flame did not come back.

'It's gone. It's really gone⋯⋯.'

Binson stared at the dead fire, stupefied and covered with ash.

Snap − . Something snapped in his heart. It was the sound of the anchor of hope he had buried deep within his heart breaking under the pouring rain.

sleepless on the island

Binson grew weak rapidly. At first he didn't have the appetite to eat, but then his stomach couldn't hold the food even if he tried to. If he forced down the food he would get a bad stomachache and constipation. Binson looked like a refugee suffering from starvation, his cheekbones jutting out from his sallow face.

With the headaches came insomnia. He couldn't sleep no matter how hard he tried. Sometimes he couldn't sleep for days on end. Even when he did doze off, he would wake up in less than 10 minutes, sweating from a nightmare. He felt dead tired but couldn't sleep, which was unbearable.

Exhausted, Binson spent most of the day lying down. It was because he felt dizzy when he tried to sit up, but the bigger problem was that he didn't have anything he wanted to do. For Binson, regaining his strength, escaping the island, or even breathing was tiresome. The wish that everything would end quickly was weighing down on Binson's languid body.

snap (동) 부러지다, 끊어지다
constipation (명) 변비
tiresome (형) 성가신, 따분한, 지겨운
languid (형) 늘어진, 맥없는
cheer up 기운을 내다
(being) stupefied and covered with ash 재를 뒤집어
　쓴 채 망연한 표정으로

the appetite to eat 먹으려는 의욕 → 식욕
even if he tried to (hold food) 대부정사라는 것이다
his cheekbones jutting out from his sallow face 앞
　에 with가 생략된 양태부사구이다
on end 연달아(= continuously). for days on end 며
　칠 동안 계속해서
weigh down 짓누르다

Why do people sleep? Scholars explain that activities of the day build up fatigue and increases sleep inducers that make a person feel sleepy. The fatigue and sleep inducer reach their height at around 11 o'clock to midnight.

Another element that causes sleepiness is the biological clock in the human body. When the morning sunlight enters the eye it stimulates the central nervous system decreasing the secretion of melatonin and wakes you up. On the other hand, when it gets dark melatonin secretion increases and makes you feel drowsy.

The state of sleep is divided into REM (Rapid Eye Movement) sleep and NREM (Non Rapid Eye Movement) sleep. During NREM sleep the heartbeat and blood pressure fall, breathing slows and the muscles relax. During REM sleep, the blood pressure is similar to that of wakening state, the heartbeat and breathing becomes irregular, but the muscles relax to a point of near paralysis.

NREM sleep is divided into 4 stages-higher stage means deeper sleep. When you first fall asleep you enter into NREM sleep then gradually move to REM sleep. This cycle is repeated every 90 minutes or so. Stages one and two of NREM sleep are light sleep, and stages three and four of NREM sleep and REM sleep are 'deep sleep.' This means you move back and forth from light to deep sleep four or five times every night.

A newborn baby's sleep is mostly REM sleep, and in about 2~6 months, NREM sleep begins. What's interesting is that the release of growth hormones reaches its peak at stage 4 of NREM sleep. The old saying 'the baby that sleeps well will grow well too' had foundation, it turns out. When a person gets into the 60s NREM sleep decreases, being unable to sleep deeply at night. Daytime naps increase also. The reason we say "sleep decreases with age" is because many older people have trouble sleeping at night.

It is widely accepted that dreams occur during REM sleep. Some scholars suggest that the eyeballs move rapidly during this state of sleep because we are following the images that appear in our dreams. On the other hand, there is also a theory that REM sleep clears the brain of unnecessary data to improve the cognitive power the next day. The exact function of REM sleep is yet to be found.

What causes sleep paralysis? The exact cause has not been found yet, but the state of sleep paralysis and REM sleep are very much alike. When you have a nightmare in the state of light sleep where the muscles are extremely relaxed, the breathing is irregular and you are vaguely awake, you feel something is pressing down on your heart and feel paralyzed.

Excessive stress and anxiety can cause insomnia like Binson's case. Unlike short-term insomnia that lasts for a few days, long-term insomnia may last for years and requires psychiatric help. According to statistics about 10% of the total population suffer from long term insomnia. On the other hand, narcolepsy or "sleep attack" (or at least a predisposition to it) is usually hereditary, but it occasionally is linked to brain damage from a head injury or neurological disease.

Argh! 1 can't see!

"Ummm⋯⋯."

Binson was tossing and turning, moaning thinly, then opened his eyes. His eyes were sunk and bloodshot, as if on a picture taken at night.

'I couldn't sleep well again last night⋯⋯.'

Binson sighed, and then realized that it was unusually quiet around him. He couldn't hear the sound of the rain that had continued for a fortnight.

"Has it stopped raining?"

Binson raised himself with an effort and looked out the window. Sunlight! A warm ray of sunlight was shining through the window. Yesterday's rough sea was now calm and serene. He could see the emerald sky above the peaceful horizon. The long, tiresome rain had finally let up. But then.

"That's odd······."

Binson rubbed his eyes, confused. He felt as if his range of vision had narrowed. First he thought it must be the sudden beam of sunlight, but no matter how many times he rubbed his eyes and opened them again, the

---

secretion (명) 분비
drowsy (형) 졸리게 하는
paralysis (명) 마비 a point of near paralysis 마비상태에 가까운 정도
release (명) 분비 the release of growth hormones 성장호르몬의 분비
nap (명) 낮잠 Daytime naps 낮잠
cognitive (형) 인지의, 인지에 관한 the cognitive power 인식력
alike (형) 비슷한. 수식할 때는 보통 much가 쓰인다
psychiatric (형) 정신의, 정신과의
narcolepsy (명) 수면 발작(= sleep attack)
predisposition (명) 병의 징후
hereditary (형) 유전성의, 유전적인

bloodshot (형) 충혈된, 핏발이 선
fortnight (명) 보름(= two weeks)
sleep inducer 수면유도체
biological clock 생체시계
becomes irregular(become + 형용사) ~하게 되다(= grow + 형용사)
or so 가량, 쯤
It is widely accepted that + 절 ~은 보편적으로 인정되는 사실이다
neurological disease 뇌질환
was tossing and turning 뒤척이다
raised himself with an effort 힘겹게 몸을 일으키다
A warm ray of sunlight 따뜻한 햇살
He felt as if ~한 듯한 느낌이었다

sea definitely looked narrower.

"Why is this happening? Is it because I lack sleep?"

Binson closed his left eye. The world seen only through his right eye looked the same as when he had both eyes opened. Then what? This time Binson closed his right eye trying not to think the worst.

'I will see. Of course I will see·······.'

But he couldn't see anything. He could only see pitch black with his left eye. Oh God! Binson's heart sank as he firmly shut his eyes.

"I can't see! Nothing was wrong until yesterday and now I'm blind······ No, this can't be. This can't be happening!"

Binson clenched his teeth. Then he slowly opened his left eye with his thumb and index fingers.

'I don't care if I see hell or even the devil himself. Please, let me see something·······.'

But what entered his retina was still only the darkness. Unfortunately his eye couldn't look at anything but the darkness now.

"I can't see······ anything."

Binson muttered as his arm dropped to his side. The world that he was seeing with the right eye began to fog. Even his left eye that could no longer see was streaming with tears.

"This can't be. Nothing's wrong with my eye!"

Binson stood up, still crying.

---

thumb (명) 엄지
retina (명) 망막. 복수형은 retinae 혹은 retinas
fog (동) 흐릿해지다, 불분명해지다
the same as ~와 똑같이

He could only see pitch black with his left eye 왼쪽
눈으로는 칠흙 같은 어둠만을 볼 수 있었다
I don't care if ~해도 개의치 않는다
Even his left eye 왼쪽 눈까지도

"It's only because I've grown weak. I will feel better when I eat. No, just some water will make me better⋯⋯."

Shouting desperately he picked up the cup at the head of the bed. But then.

"Huh?"

Binson's hand stopped in midair as he was gulping the water. He felt as if something was stuck in his throat. He tried to clear his throat but it still felt uncomfortable. It was as if a big chop of meat was blocking his gullet.

"This makes no sense. I didn't even eat anything⋯⋯."

Binson felt his throat with his fingers. But unlike the thick feeling from inside, his fingers didn't feel anything. Now he felt stifled every time he breathed, as if the lump had grown.

"What could this be? Cancer? First I get blind and now I get a lump inside my body⋯⋯."

Binson felt dizzy and sank to the cabin floor that was still wet. A sudden laugh of despair spread on Binson's lips as he sat there staring into thin air.

'What if it's cancer or it's not. I won't last long anyway⋯⋯.'

Binson had an odd look in his face, which was neither a smile nor a weep. He slowly lost his consciousness.

There are some students who are fine normally but suffer from headaches or stomachaches whenever there's an exam. Medicine doesn't help and the doctor says there's nothing wrong. It looks like feigned illness but to them it's definitely not feigned. Symptoms that are caused by anxiety, depression or stress are called psychosomatic disorders.

Psychosomatic disorders are related to the autonomous nervous system. The autonomous nervous system includes the sympathetic and parasympathetic nervous systems, and is a very important organ that affects the retina, heart, veins, sweat glands, stomach, respiratory organs and bladder. If you feel anxiety in the cerebral cortex it is transmitted through the hypothalamus to the autonomous nervous system. The autonomous nervous system is disrupted and various physical symptoms occur.

When the sympathetic nervous system is active adrenaline levels in the blood increases and sugar efflux in the liver heightens, resulting in an increase in blood pressure and pulse rate. The blood that flows to the stomach decreases causing stomachaches. Insomnia, depression, and even loss of eyesight or paralysis in the hands and feet may also occur.

The lump in the throat that Binson felt was another form of psychosomatic disorder known as globus hystericus.

Mind-body therapy that aims to cure psychosomatic disorders is one of the least advanced areas in modern medicine. As there is no definite cure, it is said the best way is for the patient to overcome anxiety or depression. As the saying 'a sound mind in a sound body' goes, so is the opposite, where the body can stay healthy only with a healthy mind.

Wake up, Binson

"Wake up, Binson……."

'Who could that be? This voice coming from afar……? I must have heard something else. It must have been the wind. There's no one on this island to call to me so gently.'

"Wake up, Binson……."

'Oh! This voice is······ yes, I'm sure now. This is mom's voice.'

Binson tried to open his eyes. But his heavy eyelids felt as if a lump of metal was hanging onto it and Binson couldn't open them.

'I have to open my eyes. I have to open them to see mom·······.'

"Wake up, Binson·······."

His eyes finally flew open. He could see a blurry image of a person standing close. Curly hair, round face and colorful skirt······ it was his mother. He had missed her so much. Binson rubbed his irritated eyes and muttered in a choked voice.

"Mom, how did you get here?"

That moment, his ears rang with a thunder.

---

desperately (부) 필사적으로
gullet (명) 목구멍
stifled (형) 숨이 막히는
dizzy (형) 현기증이 나는. feel dizzy 현기증이 나다
weep (명) 울기, 흐느낌
Symptom (명) 징후, 증상
bladder (명) 방광
hypothalamus 시상하부
efflux (명) 유출, sugar efflux 당분유출
liver (명) 간
blurry (형) 흐려진, 희미한
irritated (형) 따끔따끔한 his irritated eyes 따끔따끔 아픈
   그의 눈
choke (동) 막다, 질식시키다
at the head of the bed 침대 머리밑
makes no sense 뜻이 통하지 않다 → 말도 안돼!

cf) make sense 이해할 수 있다
every time he breathed 숨을 내쉴 때마다(= whenever
   he breathed)
What if~ ~일지라도 알게 뭐야, 상관없다
an odd look 이상한 표정
feigned illness 꾀병
psychosomatic disorders 심신장애
sympathetic and parasympathetic nervous
systems 교감신경계와 부교감신경계
cerebral cortex 대뇌 피질
globus hystericus 히스테리구(球)
it is said (that)~ = we say that~
This voice (which is) coming from afar 멀리에서 들
   려오는 이 목소리
how did you get here 어떻게 여기에 왔는가?

"Binson! Get up now! I told you three times already."

Thirty minutes had passed already since mom had started her lecture. She started digging up his faults the moment she laid eyes on him.

"Didn't I tell you to go on your trip later and stay home to study or not?"

"You did."

"If you had to go on your trip, didn't I tell you to go somewhere near or not?"

"You did."

"If you had to go far, didn't I tell you to leave another day or not?"

"You did."

"If you had to leave that day, didn't I tell you to have breakfast first and not leave by the first flight or not?"

"You did."

"If you had to take the first flight, didn't I tell you to take another airline or not?"

"You did."

"Just who do you take after to be so disobedient? If you had done one thing as I told you, this wouldn't have happened."

"I'm sorry."

"That's not all. Why did you let the fire die?"

"But I kept it going for two months······."

"Quiet! In your grandmother's time, women never let the fire die that they brought when they married and passed it on to the daughter in law. I never let the briquette go out before we had a boiler."

"I'm sorry."

"Let's suppose I go easy on you on all that. What you really did wrong was the next thing. You shouldn't have lost courage and will to survive until someone came to rescue you. You didn't even last three months. Can you still tell me you're the eldest son of the Noh family?"

"I'm sorry."

"Sigh. What can you do right except say 'I'm sorry?'"

"······ I'm sorry."

"Is everyone ok? How's dad? And my brother and sister?"

"Do you think they would be ok in this situation?"

---

disobedient (형) 반항적인, so disobedient 이렇게 말을
　듣지 않는
briquette (명) 연탄, 조개탄
dig up 발굴하다
digging up his faults 잘못을 들춰내다
the moment she laid eyes on him = as soon as she
　laid eyes on him

by the first flight 첫 비행기로
take after 닮다 = resemble
If you had done one thing as I told you, this
　wouldn't have happened = Because you didn't do
　one thing as I told you, this happened
go easy on ~을 너그러이 봐주다

Yeah, his family couldn't be doing ok. They would all probably think he was dead by now.

Suddenly he missed his family so much that his eyes watered. A sad look was on his mother's face, looking onto Binson.

"Mom, wait for me. I will come back soon."

"Don't think of anything else but getting better. You can't even stand straight, where do you think you will go in that condition?"

"Home, of course."

"Easier said than done. How do you plan to cross the sea?"

"But I can't stay here forever. You can't live without me."

"If you really care about me, stay healthy and wait for rescue. What if something happens when you go out to sea? I want you to stay safe than try anything risky."

"......"

"You will get better. Indeed. You're my son. If it gets tough, think of me. We will see each other again."

"I will, mom."

"Ok then, I'm leaving now."

"Wait, mom."

"What is it? I'm busy. I have to make lunch for your brother and sister."

"Ummmm······ is Malsuk doing ok?"

"She is doing great. She has been meeting other boys since the day you left."

"What??"

Malsuk is seeing other guys? How could she? But his mother's next words were even more shocking.

"She is seeing a young man named Chanson. Maybe she likes the name because it is the opposite of yours."

Ugh······ Binson's thick eyebrows twitched. Mom watched Binson then slowly walked backwards until she disappeared into the fog. Mom's tear was sparkling on the ground like dew.

eyebrow (명) 눈썹
by now 지금쯤
but ~이외에는
where (do you think) you will go in that condition
  do you think를 삽입절로 생각하며 번역하면 쉽다
Easier said than done 말하기는 쉬워도 실천하기는 어렵다
care about 걱정하다, 염려하다

it gets tough 힘들다, 비인칭 it
We will see each other again 우리는 다시 만날 것이다(each other가 see의 목적어 역할이다)
is Malsuk doing ok 말숙은 잘 지내나요?
the day you left? ← the day when you left, 관계부사 when 생략
walked backwards 뒷걸음질치다

Binson gets back to his feet

When Binson woke from his dream he closed his eyes again and thought back of the dream. He thought of the worried voice trying to wake him. The sight of mom walking backwards so that she could watch him for a bit longer. And the tear that was sparkling on the ground.

"Mom's right. I will get better. I will get back on my feet. I'm mom's son"

Binson clenched his fists. Now he had definite reasons to get back on his feet. He had his family waiting for him, and he had to get back at Malsuk who was seeing another guy. Binson was determined to hold out until he got rescued.

He made a fire again. He lit up the distress signal too. He cleaned up the messy cabin and went out to get fresh water. Then he made some broth to ease his stomach. He felt dizzy and his legs wobbly, but his eyes were regaining the light that had been gone. Under the rich sunlight, Binson tied the knot to his anchor of hope once again.

"One, two, three, whew − ."

Binson unclenched his fists and let out a deep breath. Then he clenched his fists again and began to count.

'One, two, three, four, five·······.'

Binson was doing a muscle relaxation exercise. He was stretching the muscles that had become tense due to stress.

It is simple to do. Sit comfortably on a chair or lie down and calm your mind. Then contract the muscles in each part of the body for 5 seconds before letting go, and repeat three times. First the fists, then arms, feet, legs, back, torso, and the face and head the last. Inhale while contracting and exhale deeply when letting go.

Binson repeated this exercise every morning and evening. And he thought of happy memories for his mental health.

He thought of the first day he met Malsuk, the times he spent with her, receiving a certificate for perfect attendance on his graduation day, the day his friends tossed him in the air congratulating him on entering the university, and how his heart raced the day he left for the trip·······.

---

messy (형) 엉망인, 지저분한
broth (명) 수프, 국
wobbly (형) 흔들거리는, 비틀대는
contract (동) 수축시키다
torso (명) 상반신, 몸통
Inhale (동) 숨을 들이마시다 (반대어: exhale)
the worried voice trying to wake him 그를 깨우려던 근심어린 목소리, 분사절의 형용사적 용법
get back on his feet 다시 일어서다

hold out 견디다, 저항하다(=endure)
was determined to V ~하기로 결심하다(= make up his mind)
He felt dizzy and his legs (felt) wobbly 동일한 동사가 생략된 형태
let out 내뱉다, 내쉬다
muscle relaxation exercise 근육이완운동
a certificate for perfect attendance 개근상

This was not that easy. Other not-so-pleasant thoughts kept interrupting. He remembered being stood up by Malsuk, and he realized that he hadn't received any other award other than perfect attendance. He felt as if his back still hurt when he remembered he had fallen while his friends were tossing him in the air. Worst of all, the terrible moment of the accident came back to him occasionally.

Whenever that happened he shook his head and shook off those memories. And he envisioned being reunited with his family. Or he imagined Malsuk kissing him in welcome. Such thoughts always brought a smile to his face.

The only thing he failed at envisioning was receiving an award. He wanted to imagine receiving an honors award at his college graduation, but no matter how hard he tried he just couldn't. After failing several times, Binson muttered, clicking his tongue.

"Yeah. That's not imagination; it's more like a delusion."

Along with his imaginations, another habit Binson worked on was thinking positively of himself. He decided he would not think of his mistakes and shortcomings but only his merits. If he was to escape from the island he had to love and trust himself completely……. It was a priceless lesson he had learned through his times of despair.

"I am good at computer games. I am a fast runner. I have a good appetite. I sleep well. And······ what else do I do well·······."

Binson thought hard about his merits.

'I am a good liar, but that's not a merit······ what else?'

After thinking for a while, Binson tapped his knee and muttered.

"Yes! I fart a lot, too."

Binson regained his vigor. His stomachache and headache eased up considerably, and insomnia got much better too. The refreshed feeling after a good night's sleep was a great source of energy for Binson. He regained his appetite too. Now he was worried he would become pot-bellied.

The lump in the throat vanished. But what made Binson happiest was that he could see with his left eye again. The darkness lifted when despair and doubt left his heart. He hadn't realized until then how bright and

---

envision (동) 상상하다 (=imagine)
delusion (명) 망상
shortcoming (명) 결점, 단점(=defect)
priceless (형) 값으로 따질 수 없는, 아주 소중한
fart (동) 방귀 뀌다
vigor (명) 원기, 기운 regained his vigor 기운을 되찾다
pot-bellied (형) 올챙이배의
lift (동) 걷히다
that (부) 그렇게(= to that extent)

Worst of all 가장 나쁜 것, 최악의 경우
an honors award 우등상
not think of his mistakes and shortcomings but only his merits not A but B의 강조형태
what made Binson happiest 빈손을 가장 행복하게 해 준 것(= what made Binson happier처럼 비교급 형태 를 써도 똑같은 뜻)
He hadn't realized until then 그때서야 비로소 ~한다는 것을 깨닫다

beautiful the world was.

Evening. The red sun was setting beyond the horizon.

Binson thought of his mother, looking at the clouds red with the sunset. And he thought of her tear that sparkled like dew.

Mom's tears. It was truly great. One drop had made hope sprout in his heart and pushed away the despair the hard rain had brought. Binson

thought that all the water of the ocean could not be more precious than one drop of his mother's tears.

Balance sheet of hope and despair

"I don't like imitating Robinson, but it's still a good idea."

Binson frowned as if he had remembered the smug expression on Robinson's face. But like he had said, it was a good idea. After all, education starts by imitating others.

"This isn't really just imitating, it's creative imitation. These days, songwriters take samples from other songs, and writers often parody others' work. Not only that. Business people do the so-called benchmarking, following others' success stories.

Who could blame me for trying something similar to what Robinson Crusoe had done?"

---

sprout (동) 생기다, 발아하다
smug (형) 잘난 체하는, 독선적인
parody (동) 모방하다
benchmarking (명) 벤치마킹
pushed away 밀어내다
all the water of the ocean could not be more

precious than one drop of his mothers tears 바닷물 전부도 어머니의 눈물 한 방울보다 값질 수 없다 → 최상급의 표현
Balance sheet 대차대조표
blame A for B B로 A를 책망하다

Just what was Binson up to? He was about to make an island balance sheet. He was going to list all the factors of hope and despair, and make them into a chart. That was what Robinson had done after about one and a half years after he was stranded on an island to look back to his past days.

"Now is the time for me to look back on my days here and summarize the situation at hand. Then I will be able to start afresh."

Binson swept the dirt floor by the cabin and picked up a twig. The ground was his notebook and twig his pencil. Although his writing material was rough, Binson's heart was calm and peaceful.

'I will write all my feelings without any sort of pretense.'

Binson's hand began to move slowly.

Binson's hand stopped. He looked down at what he had written for a long while. There were so many hopeful things in this seemingly endless pit of loneliness and despair······ He nodded and murmured quietly.

"Robinson was right. No matter how miserable the situation seems, there is always something to be thankful of. He was indeed correct."

Binson thought of ⟨Robinson Crusoe⟩ he had read some time ago.

'He had survived for 28 years because of that attitude. There's a lot to learn if it weren't for that bragging······ No. I shouldn't say that. Walls have ears. If Robinson were to hear me say this, he will get even more

 **Despair**

 Hope

I am stranded on an isolated island. I am living a miserable life, all alone.

But I didn't lose my life like other passengers on the plane. I was blessed, and I will be saved from this island.

I lack food and don't have a safe place to stay in. I have to work hard everyday to survive and always be on alert.

But I was able to get food and water and now even have some stored. I am in a much better situation than starving to death in a desert or field of gravel.

I have no strength or weapon to protect myself from ferocious animals.

But I haven't seen any animals that could be a threat to me ever since I got here.

I miss Mom. She's probably spending her days in tears.

But I see mom every night in my dreams. And I regained courage thanks to her. She will continue to be my source of strength.

I miss Malsuk. She may be having a great time with another guy, having forgotten all about me.

But I believe in Malsuk. Even if she had seen other guys, she will come back to me when I get back. Besides, no one can put up with her whims but me.

I want to get out of here. But there is no way out, and there seems to be little hope of being rescued.

But I will get out of here, because I have a family that I love, I have Malsuk, and most importantly the 21st century is waiting for me.

puffed up.'

Binson closed his mouth lest Robinson may have heard him. Then he read what he had written aloud.

"This is black-ink balance·······.'

The balance sheet on the island turned out to be in the black. Black in the name of hope.

Aloe, the marvelous herb

"Ouch!"

Binson grabbed his hand with a scream. Blood dripped between his fingers. He had cut himself trying to trim bamboo with the knife.

Binson scowled as he looked at his wound. His left finger was gaping like the gills of a fish and pouring out blood. If he were at home he would have applied a disinfectant, and ointment, and tied it up with some sterilized gauze, but there was no first aid kit on this island. Binson had only reached the early stone ages.

Binson first pressed down his finger to stop the bleeding. Then he tore the sleeve of his shirt and tied it around his finger. But the bleeding didn't stop. The piece of cloth started to stain with blood.

"Oh no. I have to stop the bleeding······."

Binson was immersed in thought with a perplexed expression. Since there was no ointment he had to find other means to stop the bleeding. What would have they done in the stone ages when someone got injured during battle or hunting? Would they have called a shaman? Would they have ground dinosaur bones and applied it to the wound······ Binson jerked his head up. His eyes shone in a long time.

"Herbs!"

Binson roamed around the woods, dripping blood from his hand. He

---

afresh (부) 새로이, 다시 start afresh 다시 시작하다
pretense (명) 거짓 꾸미기
seemingly (부)겉보기에는
loneliness (명) 외로움, 쓸쓸함
trim (동) 다듬다
scowl (동) 얼굴을 찡그리다(=frown)
gape (동) (입을) 벌이다
disinfectant (명) 소독약
ointment (명) 연고
stain (동) 얼룩지다
perplexed (형) 당혹스런 a perplexed expression 난
　감한 표정
got injured 상처를 입다, 다치다
make them into a chart 그것들을 도표화시키다

The ground was his notebook and twig (was) his pencil 동일한 동사의 생략
without any sort of pretense 손톱만큼의 꾸밈도 없이
No matter how miserable the situation seems =
　Though the situation seems very miserable
be thankful of ~에 대해 감사하게 여기다
that attitude 그런 마음가짐 → 앞의 독백
puff up 우쭐해하다
black-ink balance 흑자
with a scream 소리를 지르면서
the gills of a fish 물고기의 아가미
sterilized gauze 소독된 거즈
first aid kit 구급약품상자
roam around ~부근을 돌아니다

was looking for something to use as hemostatic. Of course he had no expert knowledge of medicinal herbs. He only knew one thing. It was that aloe was good for treating wounds. He had read it in a magazine last summer when he went to a bank to escape the heat of the day.

Fortunately he knew what aloe looked like. When in high school he had seen Malsuk covering her face with aloe leaves to cure her pimples. Green leaves on her bumpy face had really been a sight to see.

'That bumpy face turned clear and smooth. Malsuk is the true model of human victory······.'

He must have bled about a couple of cups of blood before he found a group of aloe in the neck of the woods. Sticky liquid oozed out as he

peeled the inner skin of the leaf. It was the mysterious sap that had cured Malsuk's pimples.

"Would this really stop the bleeding?"

Binson stopped in mid air while putting the shredded aloe leaves to his wound. He had suddenly remembered mom's words. When he scratched a mosquito bite when he was a kid, his mother always used to say,

"Binson, don't scratch; put some spit on it. Spit is good for wounds. I told you to stop!"

Aloe sap or spit? After some thought, he decided he would use both to be fair. He put a piece of aloe leaf in his mouth and chewed it.

'If there was some toenjang I would have mixed that too······.'

As he applied the aloe leaf mixed with his spit, it felt cool and sore at the same time. He tied the wound again and came back to his cabin with several roots of aloe. It was going to be his first aid kit.

---

hernostatic (명) 지혈제
pimple (명) 여드름
bumpy (형) 울퉁불퉁한
Sticky (형) 끈적한
sap (명) 수액(樹液)
shred (동) 잘게 자르다
sore (형) 쓰라린
medicinal herbs 약초
He only knew one thing. It was that aloe was good

for treating wounds = All he knew was that aloe~
to escape the heat of the day 대낮의 열기를 피하려고
what aloe looked like 알로에의 생김새
in the neck of the woods 숲 어귀에서
ooze out 흘러나오다(=flow out)
is good for ~에 좋다, 효과가 있다
a piece of aloe leaf 알로에 잎 조각
the aloe leaf mixed with his spit 침과 섞인 알로에 잎
　(과거분사절이 형용사 역할로 aloe leaf를 수식)

Green medicine that grow
in the woods and fields

Plants are the oldest medicine in human history. In the old days, it was believed that when someone fell ill, a plant that looked similar to that part of the body would cure the illness. A round leaf was used for the liver, a heart-shaped leaf was used for heart disease, and nuts that looked like the brain was believed to be good for headaches.

As time passed, people discovered plants that had real effect and many of those plants have become part of modern medicine. Quinine which is extracted from the bark of cinchona tree to cure malaria was found by South American natives. If it weren't for the folk medicine of boiling the bark of a willow tree to drink to treat arthritis, scientists wouldn't have found salicin, the basis of aspirin.

Even today, a large part of new drugs are made from plants. Scientists observe what the indigenous peoples use to cure wounds or diseases, and study their components.

Among the 350,000 plant species, only 10% have been tested for medical effects. The importance of plants is much more emphasized in Eastern medicine. Koreans used wild plants in the fields as medicine instead of the expensive herbal medicine sold at the clinic.

Below are some medicinal herbs that are easy to find around us.

- White dandelion: cures side effects of fevers and rashes. It also eases indigestion. It is also useful when stung by a poisonous insect, and when chewed raw it is good for gastric ulcer and chronic dyspeptic.
- Dandelion: boil dried dandelion in water and drink to lower fever, hemorrhoids, edema and indigestion. It increases bile secretion and helps at the stool.
- Thistle: crush the leaves and apply to a wound to stop the bleeding.
- Mugwort: gather in the spring, dry in the shade and drink the boiled water to cure stomachache, lumbago, asthma, and hemorrhoids. Put it in a pouch and soak in bath water to ease pain in the back and knees, and contusion.
- White bellflower: its main component is saponin, which is good for phlegm and coughs.
- Plantain: pick in the summer and dry in the shade and decoct to ease coughs, asthma, pertussis, stomach illness, diarrhea, and headaches.
- Water parsley: it is good for pyrexia and high blood pressure. Drink raw juice and boiled alternately to ease jaundice.

Binson ran with all his might. Carl Lewis or Ben Johnson couldn't have run faster than him. But then, even the fastest sprinters couldn't be in such a hurry as Binson. They were not being chased by a swarm of angry bees.

"Arghh, help!"

Binson's scream rang through the woods. He shouldn't have touched the beehive to get honey. He had thought it was empty because there were no bees flying around. But the hive was swarming with them. It started with one then they began their attack in a swarm. He had literally

stirred up a hornet's nest.

Binson was stung about ten times, then as he flew through the woods he found a brook. Water! Binson didn't think twice before jumping in. The bees wouldn't follow him there.

Binson switched from the army to the navy, and the air force withdrew their stings and flew away. Binson stuck his head out gasping for breath. His lips had swelled up bad.

"I got stung here. And there······ ugh, just how many places did I get stung?"

Binson examined the sting bites, moaning. Arms, shoulders, chest,

---

nut (명) 견과류
Quinine (명) 키니네
arthritis (명) 관절염
dandelion (명) 민들레
rash (명) 발진
hemorrhoid (명) 치질
edema (명) 부종
bile secretion 담즙의 분비
stool (명) 통변
Thistle (명) 엉겅퀴
Mugwort (명) 쑥
lumbago (명) 요통
asthma (명) 천식
contusion (명) 타박상
phlegm (명) 가래
Plantain (명) 질경이
decoct (동) 달이다
pertussis (명) 백일해

diarrhea (명) 설사
Water parsley 미나리
pyrexia (명) 열병
jaundice (명) 황달
beehive (명) 벌집, 벌통
withdraw (동) 철수하다
it was believed that ~라고 여겨지다 (= it seemed that)
the bark of cinchona tree 킨코나 나무의 껍질
If it weren't for~ ~이 없었다면
a willow tree 버드나무
indigenous peoples 원주민
gastric ulcer 위궤양
chronic dyspeptic 만성 소화불량
a swarm of ~(보통 꿀벌의) 떼
stirred up a hornet's nest 말벌의 보금자리를 들쑤시다
the air force = bees
gasping for breath 가쁜 숨을 몰아쉬며
got stung 벌에 쏘이다

navel, legs, buttocks, even the sole of his feet had been stung. It was fortunate that his face was ok, except for his lips which had become three or four times thicker.

The bee stings were quite serious. His skin turned red and swelled up from the bee venom. It was painful and terribly itchy, but Binson didn't dare scratch himself. If the wound got worse in this hot humid weather, he would really be in trouble.

Binson first sucked out the venom with his mouth and applied the aloe sap. But as marvelous the aloe sap may be, Binson doubted it could cure bee stings. And his spit wouldn't work either, because this was no mosquito bite. He needed some other medicine to get rid of the venom.

"Ammonia is best for these situations······."

Binson suddenly closed his swollen lips. Wait, ammonia? Then······ Binson bolted to his feet.

"That's it!"

"Pssss – ."

Binson made a sound as if helping a child to urinate. He had two buckets in front of him. One had water and the other was to get his urine.

"Please come out. Come out like a waterfall. Pssss – ."

Binson gulped the water and kneeled down in front of the other and puckered his swollen lips.

"Come on! I need you."

That's right. Binson was going to apply his urine in place of liquid ammonia. As the saying goes, he had learned to 'use the gums when he had no teeth'. Now that philosophy had advanced into pharmacy. The marvel drug to cure bee poisoning was – yes, urine.

The water bucket was almost empty. The other bucket on the other hand was almost full. He was disappointed that the input and output were not the same, but at least it should be enough for one day. The remaining amount will come in time, anyway.

Binson took off his clothes. Then he soaked the cloth in the urine. A not-so-pleasant odor hit his nostrils but that was only the smell of medication. He laid the cloth on the stings taking care not to drop any of the precious liquid. Binson sighed in regret.

"I should have saved some while I could."

---

navel (명) 배꼽
buttock (명) 엉덩이
itchy (형) 가려운, 근지러운
urinate (동) 오줌을 누다
pucker (동) 오므리다
nostril (명) 콧구멍
the sole of his feet 발바닥
bee venom 벌독

get rid of ~을 제거하다
the other = the bucket filled with urine
in place of ~대신에(= in stead of)
As the saying goes 속담에 있듯이
to use the gums when he had no teeth 이가 없을 때
　는 잇몸을 사용
in time 적시에, 제때에
the smell of medication 약냄새

5

Three months have passed

The sea was empty today like it had always been. Binson's hope that another ship would pass by someday was crushed again today. Maybe the ship he had seen last time had strayed away from its normal route. Or it might have been a pirate ship or a smuggling vessel. If that were the case, then no ship would pass by again.

Binson stood up with a sullen face. It had grown too dark to watch the

---

sullen (형) 시무룩한
Binson' s hope = that another ship would pass by someday
stray away 길을 잃고 표류하다

smuggling vessel 밀수선
It had grown too dark to watch the sea 너무 어두워져서 바다를 볼 수 없었다

sea.

'If no ship will pass then I'll have to count on an airplane⋯⋯.'

But the chances a plane would fly above the island were slim. At least he had seen a ship pass by, but he had never seen an airplane.

Binson came back to the cabin and counted the markings he had made on the pillar. He had made markings including the few days before building the cabin, and there were 17 of the 5-line markings. That meant 85 days. It had already been almost three months since he had been stranded on this uninhabited island.

"Soon it will be a hundred days. Should I throw a party⋯⋯?"

Binson sighed as he drew another line on the pillar. The eighty-sixth day was closing to an end.

Mirage on the sea

Binson raised his hand to wipe his ticklish mouth. Then he frowned and opened his eyes. There was a clear, sticky liquid around the mouth and on his hand.

"Ugh! What's this? It's saliva. Guess I'm finished now. I've been dribbling while dozing."

Binson wiped his mouth again, clicking his tongue. Then he wiped his hand on the sand on the hill. He thought of how he must have looked, dozing off on the hill dribbling. Binson blinked his bleary eyes, thankful that Malsuk wasn't here to see that. The midday's sun was scorching the sea and the sand.

That moment, Binson's eyes flickered strangely. He saw something vaguely in the distant sea. It wasn't a bird or a plane, and it wasn't a UFO, either. Binson sat there looking at the object, then bolted to his feet shouting.

"That's······ that's a ship!"

A ship? In mid air? And how could it be hovering like that, up side down? It wasn't the pirate spaceship in ⟨Galaxy Express 999⟩.

Binson stood there staring into the air, as if he couldn't believe what he had seen with his own eyes. But no matter how many times he looked

---

ticklish (형) 간지러운, 근질근질한
dribble (동) 침을 질질 흘리다
bleary (형) 흐릿한 his bleary eyes 게슴츠레한 눈
scorch (동) 뜨겁게 달구다
hover (동) 날다
the chances = a plane would fly above the island. that
  이 생략된 경우

throw a party 파티를 벌이다
Binson sighed as he drew another line on the pillar
  = Binson sighed drawing another line on the pillar
how he must have looked 그가 어떤 모습으로 보였을
  까
up side down 거꾸로, 뒤집어져서

again, the ship was upside down. And it wasn't a pirate ship or phantom ship. It looked like a large freighter commonly seen in pictures.

'Ugh······.'

Binson shook his head.

'What's going on? Am I still sleeping?"

"One, two, three······ eight, nine."

Binson closed his eyes and started counting. He was going to open his eyes at ten. If he had seen a hallucination, it would have gone by then.

But what if the ship was still there? What then? Binson began to feel uneasy. If the ship disappeared all would be fine, but if it didn't, something was wrong either with him or the world. And it was much more probable that the problem would be with him rather than the whole world.

"Nine and a half, almost ten······ te~n······."

Ok. He inhaled deeply and opened his eyes. And he glared at the spot where the ship had been hovering. Then he muttered in relief.

"Of course. It's gone."

Only the wind was left in the empty space.

Binson's hair that had grown long got ruffled in the wind.

All through that night he wondered what the ship could have been. A phantom ship? An apparition? UFO? But as much as he liked comics Binson could not believe that such things could really happen in reality.

'Then just what is it······.'

After endless reasoning, Binson's eye sparkled when it was almost daybreak. He mumbled, looking at the sky starting to lighten.

"That was a mirage."

---

freighter 화물선
hallucination (명) 환상, 환영
apparition (명) 유령
daybreak (명) 새벽, when it was almost daybreak
　새벽녘에야
by then 그때쯤
what if ~라면 어떻게 될까?

feel uneasy 불안해지다
glare at ~을 뚫어지게 쳐다보다
the spot where the ship had been hovering 관계부
　사절의 사용, 이때 where = over which
get ruffled 헝클어지다
as much as ~이기는 하지만(=although)

There's nothing much to
a mirage, after all

You were sure you saw it but once you get there it's gone. A mirage that is often seen on a desert or ocean and confuses people is caused by the refraction of light. The difference in the density and temperature of the air causes light's refraction and creates a fake image in the air.

The density and temperature are inversely proportional. When the air temperature rises it expands and the density decreases whereas when the temperature drops the air contracts and increases in density. In the border surface where the air density changes the light that passes through bends, and the bigger the difference in density, the bigger the refractive power.

In the sea, the cool air close to the water is denser than the warm air above. The light reflected from the ship refracts at the surface where the cool and cold air meet, causing 'total reflection.' Total reflection occurs when the angle of incidence is greater than a certain limiting angle. The ray of light in a medium of higher index of refraction approaches another medium of lower index of refraction but it does not enter into the latter and is totally reflected. When the ray from total reflection meets the eye, it looks as though the ship is hovering in mid air. That was what Binson had seen.

On the other hand, on a desert, the air close to the ground is warmer. A ray reflected from afar refracts upwards before it reaches the ground and is reflected in another place. In the summer where cars and trees above hot asphalt appear to be floating on water is caused by this phenomenon too. In 1798 Napoleon's army were scared out of their wits when the lake they had seen suddenly disappeared. A French mathematician G. Monge is known to have proved that this phenomenon was caused by the hot air of the desert. A mirage that looks so fascinating is just a natural phenomenon when you know the scientific principle behind it.

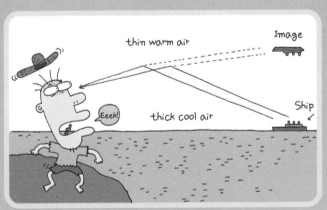

<How a mirage works>

Morning. Binson sat on the hill thinking, even forgetting to eat. At his feet were some drawings he had scribbled. He had drawn how a mirage occurs based on his memory on a science comic he had read some time ago.

"A mirage is a fake image but it doesn't appear out of nowhere. It appeared because a ship passed by somewhere. That means a ship had passed by over there······."

That was right. Binson wasn't thinking about the fake image, but the real object that had created that image.

Binson cannot see a ship that passes beyond the horizon. But he can see the mirage. Mirage on the sea is caused by the light that is refracted on it's way up.

What if a ship had passed beyond the horizon? That was both good and bad news. It was good because ships are passing by not far away. But it is also bad news because Binson can't see the ship and the ship cannot see him. Binson looked far at the sea and muttered softly.

"If only I could go as far as that horizon······."

All day long, Binson sat on the hill looking at the sea where he had seen the mirage. He hoped that this time he might see a real ship, not a mirage. But the ship didn't appear again, and another day was closing to an end.

Night. Binson got up slowly. His knees and ankles ached because he hadn't budged from where he was sitting.

'Damn mirages. I wouldn't feel so bad if I hadn't seen it in the first place……'

Binson was mumbling as he glanced at the sea again, when he stopped in mid air. His eyes began to sparkle like when he had seen the mirage of the ship.

"What's that?"

His eyes were fixed on the horizon. A part of the sky seemed a bit brighter than the rest. It was like the sky above a baseball stadium on a game night. It had been two months since he had built the cabin on the

---

refraction (명) 굴절
refract (동) 굴절하다
incidence (명) 입사. the angle of incidence 입사각
scribble (동) 휘갈겨 쓰다
budge (동) 움직이다
mumble (동) 중얼거리다
it's gone 사라지고 없다
fake image 허상
be inversely proportional 반비례하다
The light reflected from the ship 배에서 반사된 빛
be scared 두려움에 떨다
out of their wits 이성을 잃고, 제정신을 잃고

is known to V ~으로 유명하다
based on his memory 기억을 되살려서
appear out of nowhere 어디선지 모르게 나타나다
beyond the horizon 수평선 너머에
on it's way up 올라가는 중에
If only ~한다면 좋으련만
All day long 하루종일
another day was closing to an end 다시 하루가 저물어가고 있었다
from where he was sitting 그가 앉아 있던 곳에서
a bit brighter 조금 더 밝은. a bit는 비교급을 수식하는 부사구

hill, but this was the first time he noticed this. He had returned to the cabin when it got too dark to see properly.

"Could that be light? Or is it just a cloud?"

It could have been light or not. But Binson wanted to believe it was light. If that was light, it meant one of two things. There must be land beyond the horizon where people lived, or there were ships passing with their lights on. Binson's heart began to race.

'There could be people close by⋯⋯.'

Binson tossed and turned in bed again that night. His heart felt fluttery and agitated.

Morning. Binson ran to the hill with daybreak. The light sky he had seen last night had made him forget hunger or sleep. His eyes were fixed on the horizon and it was his second day to stay glued on the hill like a statue.

But the sea was calm. One hour, two hours, three hours⋯⋯ Time passed slowly and Binson's eyelids could not help feeling heavy.

Birds flew above the sea. They flew to the island shores then disappeared beyond the horizon again.

'You're lucky. You can see what is beyond the horizon. I won't eat you if you tell me⋯⋯.'

Binson was mumbling at the birds flying away when he jerked his head up. There was no trace of drowsiness in his eyes.

"Why do birds always fly that way?"

Why do they fly away? Because they have wings, of course.

But why do they always fly in the same direction? Because they like it? Or they don't know any other way? But birds don't have fixed routes in the sky like planes do. Then what? Binson slapped his knee and stood up, howling.

"There is land! There is!"

He had realized this for the first time. Birds needed some place to rest their wings too. They cannot stay in the air all day. That means somewhere beyond the horizon there's a place where birds can come down and sit. Whether it was land, island or even an uninhabited island like this one, there was sure to be land over there.

Binson had no doubts now. The mirage, the vague light in the night sky, and the birds. These three things were telling him one thing. There was land. There was land where people could live beyond that horizon. It was so clear to him. The only problem was the sea in between.

If the sea were the land······ But it was no time to idly hum the lyrics to a song. If there was land over the horizon, he had to get there by all means. If he couldn't walk there, he had to swim or even fly. Binson clenched his fists.

"I will make a raft. And I will go out to sea. That's the only way. If land cannot come to me, I will go to the land. If they can't see me, I'll go where they can. I don't care if they are cannibals or aliens. If only I can meet someone······."

Binson finally sat down again. His heart felt as if it was about to burst.

Making a raft

To make a raft, he first had to pick the right wood. He wanted to make a firm raft of thick, sturdy wood, but he had no means to transport the log. If there was a river he could float them downriver but the brook in the forest was too narrow and shallow. Unless he was going to make a boat out of leaves of course.

Finally, Binson decided to use bamboo instead of logs. He remembered seeing in a comic book where Chinese warriors traveled upstream on bamboo rafts. Bamboo is light and thin and is easy to carry, and is sturdy compared to its size, and won't break easily in the sea.

There was plenty of thick, tall bamboo. He picked the sturdiest of them, chopped them with his stone axe and moved them to the shore. He placed short bamboo on the sides and the longer ones in the middle so that the shape of the raft was streamlined. It was to minimize the resistance of water.

He twisted several thick vines and tightly tied the bamboo together. In the center of the raft he placed two thick, straight bamboo sticks about 10 meters long to use as mast. He weaved broad, tough leaves and tied it to

---

raft (명) 뗏목
warrior (명) 전사, 무사
streamline (동) 유선형으로 하다
mast (명) 돛대
weave (동) 엮다, 짜다
had no doubts 의심하지 않다 → 확신하다
the vague light 희미한 빛
the sea in between (two lands) 사이에 있는 바다
it was no time to V ~할 때가 아니다

by all means 온갖 수단을 다해서, 어떤 수를 써서라도
I don't care if~ ~하더라도 개의치 않다
was about to V = be going to V
of thick, sturdy wood 굵고 단단한 나무로 만든, 재료의 of
traveled upstream 상류로 거슬러 올라가다
compared to its size 크기에 비해서
the resistance of water 물의 저항
about 10 meters long 약 10미터 길이

the mast. If the wind blew too hard the sail would tear, but it would hold otherwise.

After cutting, carrying and tying scores of bamboo, his raft was finally complete. It looked sturdy enough not to break or tip over, unless a typhoon came. Binson looked at the raft satisfied.

"I could even play soccer on it."

But he couldn't start off to sea just because the raft was ready. He could not set the direction properly if the tide or wind pushed him in the wrong place. He could end up lost in the sea without being able to return to the island. As tired as he was of the island, it was better than having to live on a raft.

"If there's no rudder at least I need an oar."

Binson chopped a thick tree, split it vertically and began to carve a long, flat oar. Making an oar with just a stone axe and stone knife was much more difficult than making the raft. By the time he had completed two oars after days of hard work, there were more than a dozen defective oars tossed away on the ground.

Finally his preparations were complete. Now all he had to do was wait for good weather, and set out. Of course it was risky but he couldn't just sit there. At least he had to check if there was land nearby or not.

'Soon I am going over the horizon on this raft.'

Binson sat on the raft looking up at the night sky, his eyes sparkling with anticipation and hope. The sunset looked clearer than ever.

Learning to forecast weather

"Eek! Do I hear rain?"

Binson bolted outside from the cabin as he was preparing food and water for sailing. The sky had been clear until that morning and now big rain drops were falling.

'Today's not the day to set sail, I guess.'

Binson muttered disappointedly.

"I will go tomorrow. The world won't end today."

---

sail (명) 돛
otherwise 그렇지 않으면(= If the wind didn't blow too hard)
rudder (명) 조종간, 키
oar (명) 노
defective (형) 불량한, 결점 투성이의
disappointedly (부) 실망해서

tip over 뒤집어지다
end up lost in the sea 바다에서 방향을 잃다
As tired as he was of the island = though he was very tired of the island
By the time ~했을쯤
with anticipation and hope 기대와 희망으로
than ever 그 어느 때보다, 유난히

The next day. It wasn't raining and the sky was clear. It was hot and humid, and not a stir of wind could he feel. Binson went through his preparations once again then floated the raft on the water. The raft glided smoothly on the water as if to pay homage to the hard work Binson had put into it.

The raft began to wobble as he got further from the shore. But that wasn't a problem for Binson. His hope of meeting a ship was far greater than his fear. As if to show the spirit of the man of the sea, he sang in a baritone.

"Rock, rock the boat, the boat is leaving~."

That moment a cold drop of water hit Binson on the forehead. What's this? Puzzled, Binson looked up at the sky. This time another drop fell right into his nostril.

"Achoo!"

Raindrops pattered down as if to sing in harmony to Binson's sneeze. It was a shower in the middle of the sea.

Being at sea in the rain was scarier than he had thought. The sky suddenly grew dark and the waves shook the raft roughly. Scared, Binson rowed with all his strength and returned to the island. The sky must be jealous of Binson's escape.

Two days later. Binson woke up to the loud croaking of frogs by the brook.

'Today I will go over the horizon no matter what.'

But that day he met rain only a few hundred yards from the shore and had to come back again.

"How can this be? Is the rainy season starting again?"

Binson went out to the tidal flat, complaining at the sky for not cooperating. But he didn't find anything good to eat, only some jellyfish in the shallow waters. Binson came back to the cabin and lay down, not even eating supper. All the while mumbling something about luck not being good today.

"Hey Binson. Did you eat?"

Robinson approached with a smug grin.

'I thought you had moved because you didn't show up for a long

time, but here you are again.'

Binson nodded his head in his direction grudgingly. He had to keep his manners even though he didn't like him.

"Binson, want me to pop a question?"

"What?"

"What do you call a fool who sets out to sea in the rain?"

"?"

"I'll tell you. You call him Nobinson. Muhahaha! Funny, eh?"

'You, you⋯⋯.'

Binson got angry. Rubbing salt into an open wound should have its limits, thought Binson. He comes here teasing me when I'm feeling low because of the rain? Binson glared at him and retorted.

"I can't change what the sky is doing. And there's no weather forecast here either."

"Even if there were, you wouldn't know it."

Binson's thick eyebrows twitched. But Robinson went on, not minding Binson's scowl.

"Listen carefully. If the sunset is clearer than usual it means rain the next day. On a windless day, there will be a shower.

When frogs come out by the brook it means the day will be gloomy. These are all what you saw and heard for the last three days. You still want to argue there's no weather forecast here?"

"......"

"You want to know something else? You saw jellyfish earlier today didn't you?"

"So what?"

"If the jellyfish come close to shore, it means a storm is coming. If

---

manner (명) 복수로 쓰여, 예절
pop (동) 던지다
retort (동) 쏘아부치다. 되받아치다
twitch (동) 꿈틀거리다, 실룩 움직이다

gloomy (형) 흐린, 우중충한
in his direction 그의 쪽으로
I'm feeling low 기분이 좋지 않다. 저기압이다
not minding ~을 개의치 않으면서

you float that little raft tomorrow it will become like the jellyfish, is what I want to say."

"Grunt – ."

Binson moaned softly.

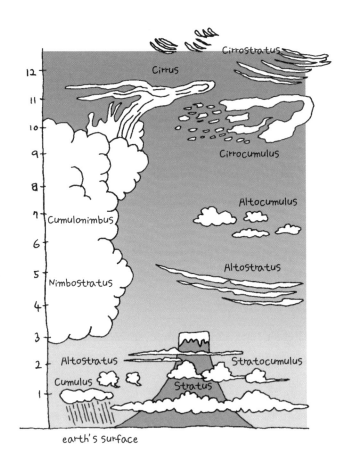

earth's surface

'According to my experience Robinson is a snob but he doesn't lie. Then? Does this mean I can't go out to sea?'

Looking at Binson's depressed face, Robinson clicked his tongue.

"You really are stupid."

"Why?"

"Think about it. If you can tell when it will rain, you can also tell when it won't……."

That moment, Binson shouted in a thunderous voice.

"Tell me!"

"No."

"Robinson, tell me please! Boo hoo − ."

Robinson put on a look of anguish. Then he consented as if doing Binson a great favor.

"Not for free."

---

snob (명) 속물
consent ~에 응하다
go out to sea 바다로 나가다

a look of anguish 고뇌에 찬 표정
doing Binson a great favor 빈손에게 큰 은혜를 베풀다
Not for free 공짜로는 안 돼

You can tell good weather by the clouds

TV or radio is not the only place to look for a weather forecast. A relatively accurate forecast is possible if you pay close attention to natural phenomena. The surest way is to observe the clouds. The altitude and shape of the clouds will enable you to make forecasts like the weather center.

High clouds

- Cirrus: the highest cloud. It appears at about 12 kilometers above ground and looks as if combed. If it is curly it predicts clear weather, and if it is radial or shaped like a belt it will turn into a rain cloud.
- Cirrostratus: it forms below cirrus clouds. It looks like a sheet in the sky. This forms a corona around the sun or the moon and is usually taken as sign of rain to come.
- Cirrocumulus: it forms right above or beneath cirrostratus. It looks like the scales of a fish, or white shells placed in the sky. If

it is seen at the shore during winter, it is sign of rain.

Middle clouds

- Altocumulus: rounded and grouped together like a flock of sheep. Forms a few kilometers below cirrocumulus clouds. If the size grows the weather will clear up and if it shrinks the weather will turn for the worse.
- Altostratus: spreads in the sky like a white awning. When it is thin the sky looks like a dim moonlit night. If it becomes thick or hangs low, it will become cloudy or rain.
- Nimbostratus: it covers the sky with no distinct feature. Brings rain or snow.

Low clouds

- Stratocumulus: appears in layers in the shape of waves, and you can see the clear sky through them. All the clouds seen when flying in an airplane are stratocumulus clouds. If the cumulus clouds turn into stratocumulus clouds at dusk it will be clear the next day. In the opposite case, it will rain the next day.

- Stratus: it appears at altitudes 1kilometer or lower and looks like a fog in mid air, and is layered. If it forms in the morning and disappears by midday the weather will be clear. But if it surrounds the mid slope of a mountain or valley below the altostratus, it will rain.

Vertical clouds

- Cumulus: puffy in a clear sky. If it disperses and disappears in the evening the weather will be clear the next day. But if it remains late into the night or drifts northwest it is sign of rain.
- Cumulonimbus: very tall cloud that can span from 1kilometer and continue up to as high as the cirrus clouds. Often accompanies heavy rain, thunder and lightning.

"Robinson was right. The weather is great today."

Binson eased the raft in the water with a satisfied look on his face, then started to row forward. The sea where storm had passed was as calm and peaceful as glass. The sail made from leaves flapped pleasantly to the moderate wind.

Binson closed his eyes. Past days flashed through his mind. The first morning he had opened his eyes on the shore. The thirst he felt while sipping on the few drops of dew. The joy he felt when he first made a fire. The coziness he felt the first night in the cabin. And the despair he had felt during the rain and the hope mom had rekindled in him······ At this moment, all those hard times seemed beautiful as if in a dream.

---

altitude (명) 고도, 높이
radial (형) 방사상의
shrink (동) 줄어들다, 위축되다
awning (명) 차양, 차일
puffy (형) 부푼, 오동통한
row (동) 노를 젓다
coziness (명) 아늑함
rekindle (동) 다시 불을 붙이다

look for 예상하다, 기다리다
pay close attention to natural phenomena 자연현상
  을 주의깊게 관찰하다
the scales of a fish 물고기의 비늘
The sail made from leaves 잎으로 만든 돛
flapped pleasantly to the moderate wind 온화한 바
  람을 받아 기분좋게 펄럭이다
as if in a dream 꿈을 꾸는 것처럼

'When I meet someone and return home, I will still come and visit this place again. With mom, Malsuk and friends. No. Maybe I should come alone like I am now. It will be an unforgettable part of my memory at age twenty.'

But what if there's nothing beyond the horizon? Still Binson would not be disappointed. He knew that courage and hope were more important than escape. Even if he didn't find land he would continue his life on the island. And some day he would talk of his adventures in his youth.

'Where will I be tonight? Will I be standing on new land with other people? Or will I be spending another lonely night alone on the island?'

Binson shook these thoughts from his head. What lonely night! He had no luxury to feel lonely now. If he didn't find land today he had to go in another direction tomorrow. And another direction the day after tomorrow. If the sun sets too soon, he would even build a lighthouse on top of the mountain on the island.

Then someday his wish will be granted. After all, hadn't he been blessed with life on the island when the plane had crashed?

'Mom, wait just a while longer. I am now getting closer to you. Malsuk, wait for me. I will kiss you for ten minutes.'

In the middle of the vast sea, he looked back. The island that had brought him both despair and hope during the last 100 days was growing distant. Some waterfowls flew above him, honking.

Still (부) 그래도
lighthouse (명) 등대
grant (동) 인정하다
waterfowl (동) 물새
honk (동) 울다, 끼룩거리다

what if theres nothing beyond the horizon? 수평선 너머에 아무 것도 없다면 어떻게 하지?
had no luxury to V ~할 만한 여유가 없다
look back 뒤돌아보다